Wild Devotion

Wilder Irish, book three

Mari Carr

ISBN: 978-1-950870-08-0

Editor: Kelli Collins

Cover artist: Melissa Gill Designs

Print formatting: Mari Carr

Life isn't measured in time. It's measured in moments...

Padraig is a carefree bartender, filled with hopes and dreams for his future…which are thrown off course when Mia walks into the bar. When she leaves in tears, Padraig follows. He hopes to give the young woman comfort and assurance. What he gets in return is a massive dose of reality.

Mia has an inoperable tumor with a diagnosis of only six months to live. As Padraig listens to her detail the things she'll never get to experience, he's forced to face some hard facts about the way he's lived his own life.

An evening of soul-searching leads to a life-changing decision—Padraig will help Mia accomplish everything on her bucket list. But that goal changes into something far deeper when Padraig falls in love with her.

Previously titled March Wind.

Dedication

This story is dedicated to all the dreamers.
Dream big.
Then go chase them.

Prologue

"Turn off the television, lad. It's time for bed."

Padraig groaned, prompting Patrick to grin. The six-year-old boy's twin brother, Colm, had fallen asleep nearly an hour earlier, but Padraig was tireless.

"Just a little longer, Pop Pop. Please."

"You asked for more time an hour ago. It's already way past your bedtime, and your mother will have both our heads if you wake up grumpy from not enough sleep."

"I'll be good tomorrow. Honest."

"Come on, Paddy. I'll tell you a story."

Padraig rolled his eyes. "Stories are dumb." He pointed to the cartoon he was watching on TV. There were a bunch of babies getting up to mischief. Patrick simply couldn't understand the appeal, but his grandchildren loved it.

"What's that show called again?" Patrick asked.

"*Rugrats*."

"Sounds about right. Come on, rugrat. I'm going to prove to you that stories aren't dumb."

Padraig begrudgingly turned off the television, and the two of them climbed the stairs to the room Padraig's father, Tris, had shared with his brother Killian when they were growing up.

Padraig and Colm had begged their parents earlier to spend the night, something they'd been asking to do more and more lately. Patrick suspected it was because he was more lenient with bedtimes and tended to indulge their requests for junk food. However, as the grandfather, that was his God-given duty. It pleased him to be able to spoil his grandkids.

It didn't hurt that these little sleepovers gave Tris and Lane a night off from their rambunctious, energetic twins. It allowed Patrick a chance to spoil *them* as well.

Padraig crawled into the twin bed, scooting over to allow him room to sit next to him. They both lowered their voices to almost whispers, as Colm was sleeping soundly in the other bed.

"This is a story about a boy named Padraig."

"Like me?" Padraig asked. The small lad took great pride in his name, and Patrick hoped he always felt that way.

"Yes. A long time ago, Ireland was a magical place filled with fairies and unicorns. Padraig was there as well, and he played a flute."

"Was it magic?" Padraig asked, his eyes wide.

"Not at the beginning, but…well, I'm getting ahead of myself. I'll get to that. Padraig loved where he lived very much, but there was one problem. Snakes."

While Padraig thought the magic was cool, his love for snakes was on an entirely different level.

"What kind of snakes? Rattlesnakes? Boa constrictors? Pythons?"

Patrick had to admit he was probably to blame for Padraig's fascination with all things that slithered. He'd taken the twins to the Maryland Zoo a few months earlier, and they'd spent quite a bit of time studying the reptiles. Since then, Padraig had checked out every snake book in the library, much to his mother's dismay, and never failed to find programs on the Discovery Channel about the creatures. Lately, he'd been begging

7

for a pet snake for Christmas, but hell would freeze over before Lane allowed that.

"The snakes in Ireland were not so deadly. Let's just say they were black snakes. The problem was there were just too darn many of them. They were everywhere. Slithering along the streets, in the crops, hiding in people's beds."

Padraig drew his feet up, tucking them under his butt with a grin.

Patrick laughed at his grandson's animated look of horror. He ruffled Padraig's hair.

"One day, the king had had enough, and he decided that the person who could get rid of all the snakes could marry his daughter."

Padraig crinkled his nose. "That's a dumb prize. I'd rather have a BB gun or a scooter."

"Well now, I wouldn't say it was such a bad reward. After all, the princess, Maureen, was very pretty, with long red hair and big green eyes. Everyone in Ireland loved her because she was sweet and kind and gentle. A lot like your mom. Padraig thought she was lovely and knew there was really nothing he wouldn't do to claim her hand in marriage."

"Did he get rid of the snakes?" Padraig was clearly unimpressed by the girl and ready to get back to the good stuff.

"He tried, along with a bunch of other men. They all wanted to earn Maureen's love. But every single one of them failed. Then one afternoon, Padraig was sitting alone in a field, playing his flute when all of a sudden a leprechaun appeared, a lively little man named Seamus. He had a flute as well."

"His was the magic one!" Padraig said, his voice loud in the quiet room.

Patrick nodded. "Shh," he warned, lest they wake up Colm. He lowered his voice even more. "Padraig caught Seamus, which was a very hard thing to do because they're so small and quick, you see. Anyway, once a leprechaun is caught, they must take you to their gold. Only Seamus didn't have any gold, so he gave his magic flute to Padraig and told him to play a marching song. Padraig did, and when he turned around, do you know what he saw?"

"What?" Padraig was clearly enthralled by the story.

"Snakes. They were following him. So Padraig kept playing and marching, and as he went, more and more snakes joined the strange parade. Padraig marched all the way to the ocean, and when he got there, he borrowed a boat, hopped on and kept playing. Do you know what those snakes did?"

Padraig shook his head.

"They followed him straight into the ocean, where they were all washed away by the waves. No more snakes in Ireland. Padraig had driven them all out. And when the king heard what he'd done, he brought Maureen to Padraig and she took one look at him, saw that he was a good man with a big heart, and she fell in love with him right on the spot. They got married and lived happily ever after."

Padraig yawned and slid down the bed, burrowing under the covers.

Patrick stood up to tuck him in, pressing a kiss to his forehead. "Do you still think stories are dumb?"

"That one was alright," Padraig replied sleepily. "I like the part about the snakes and the leprechaun."

"But not the girl?" Patrick teased.

Padraig revised his previous statement. "Girls are dumb."

"I suspect you won't always think so. And when you decide they aren't dumb, you can drive away snakes to earn her love."

Padraig closed his eyes as he twisted to his side, sleep coming fast to claim him. "I'd rather have a scooter," he said through a large yawn.

"Good night." Patrick tiptoed to the door, then turned around to look at his grandsons. While they were both rough-and-tumble boys—bulls in a china closet, he liked to say—they had big hearts.

"These two are going to be heartbreakers, sweetheart," he murmured to Sunday, his beloved wife, certain his personal guardian angel was always listening from heaven. "Going to have to trust you'll find women who are worthy of them. And patient," he added with a chuckle. "They'll definitely have to be patient women. Preferably ones who like snakes."

Chapter One

March 28

Padraig Collins glanced up when the front door of Pat's Pub opened, sending a gust of the coldest air the Inner Harbor could produce into the bar. It knocked the temperature inside down another degree or three. Mia Curtis made her way to the bar, took off her heavy coat and hung it on the back of her usual stool. He waved and pointed at the tray of drinks in his hand, indicating he'd be with her in just a second.

Of course, it was more than a second, as the older couple at the table wanted to make small talk about the "damn cold weather" and how March had come in like a lion and was going out as one, as well. They were just a few days away from April, but no one could tell that from the frigid wind that seemed to blow nonstop.

After a murmured "I hear you" and "you're so right about that," he returned to the bar, stopping first to check on the other two tables of customers. Business was slower than usual, probably because nobody wanted to risk frostbite just for a draft beer.

He snuck a quick peek at Mia as one of the tables requested their check. She'd moved to Baltimore four months earlier, renting an apartment across the cobblestone street from the pub. She'd only been in the city a few days when she'd ventured over to Pat's Pub for dinner.

As seemed to be the habit of most lonely souls, she'd opted for a spot at the end of the long mahogany bar rather than claiming a table of her own. Padraig was used to making small talk with folks who came in to dine alone, and Mia had been no exception.

Since that first night, she'd come over once or twice a week for dinner and he always enjoyed her company.

Padraig smiled as he walked behind the counter. As he made his way down the bar to her, he poured her a glass of Chardonnay, her usual order. She wasn't looking at him, but instead she was staring at the counter, very deep in thought.

"You're a brave soul."

She jerked at the sound of his voice, and he realized she really *had* to be distracted, not to notice him standing right in front of her.

"What?" she asked.

"I said you're a brave soul. To venture out in this godforsaken March wind. You're one of the few."

She nodded, but didn't reply.

Padraig frowned. It wasn't like her not to hop in on any conversation. He tried again. "Let me guess. There's no food in your house and you're here in search of dinner. Tonight's special is—"

"I don't think I'm eating."

"Oh. Okay. You feeling alright?"

"Yeah."

As far as reassurances went, Padraig was fairly certain that was the worst in history. Something was obviously bothering her, but Padraig didn't feel right prying. It wasn't like they were friends. In truth, apart from the innocuous conversations they had about sports, the weather and his tips on how to survive in Baltimore as she ate her dinner, he didn't know much about Mia.

"Well, tell you what. Why don't you wave me over if you decide you want some food?"

She nodded, but she was already looking away, her eyes distant as whatever was bothering her crept back in.

Padraig tidied up the bar, poured another round for his cousin, Finn, who was indulging in an extended happy hour with some of his friends, and snuck more than a few glances at the hockey game playing on one of several televisions in the bar.

Through it all, Mia sat at the counter without speaking, her wine untouched.

He left her alone for nearly forty-five minutes before he broke. He possessed more than his fair share of Collins blood, which meant it wasn't in his genetic makeup to let anyone be sad in his presence.

Besides, he'd caught several unguarded expressions, and while he didn't know what was wrong, he could tell it was big.

"Only got a couple more weeks until the Stanley Cup playoffs. Caps are going all the way this year." He figured that would jerk her out of her depression. Mia, a Chicago native, was nothing if not loyal to her Blackhawks.

"Cool."

He frowned at her distracted response. He tried again. "Blackhawks don't stand a chance this year. Loaded the bench with too many showboats. Bunch of damn cherry pickers and no defense."

She nodded, and he realized she wasn't listening to him.

He leaned down, resting his elbows on the bar so that his face was level with hers. He waited until she lifted her downcast gaze and met his. Again, he got the sense she was startled to see him there.

"Caps own the ice this year," he said, trying once more to evoke a response.

"Okay." The words were little more than a whisper.

He narrowed his eyes. "What's wrong, Mia?"

For the first time, his words penetrated. Unfortunately, not in a great way. Her green eyes filled with tears that she tried desperately to blink away.

"I shouldn't have come here. I just…"

"What is it?" he prodded, his concern growing. While Mia was essentially a stranger, his protective instincts rose to the forefront.

"I should go." She dug in her purse for her wallet to pay for the wine, but he waved her away.

"Don't worry about it," he said. "You didn't drink it."

"But—"

"You didn't even order it. I'm not taking your money, Mia."

She put her wallet away and stood, shrugging on her heavy coat. Padraig studied her face more closely as she did so. She was pale and there were dark circles under her eyes. Her body was rigid, and he got the sense she was just barely holding herself together.

He tried again. "If you need someone to talk to…"

Mia looked up at him and for a second, he thought she might take him up on the offer. Her mouth opened as if to speak, but then she closed it again, swallowing heavily.

Padraig felt helpless to comfort her, something he didn't experience often. He sort of prided himself on his ability to cheer people up. God knew, as a bartender, he'd had plenty of opportunities to hone that skill over the past ten years. He'd started working at the pub during high school. Unlike his twin brother, Colm, school was not his thing. Over the years, he'd bussed tables, then waited them, and once he hit twenty-one, his dad, Tris, taught him everything there was to know about mixing drinks.

Dad had always run the pub side of Pat's Pub with Aunt Kiera and Ewan managing Sunday's Side. Padraig had only been tending bar a couple of years when his father decided the two of them should split the head bartender duties. His dad held the reins during the daylight hours and Padraig took over at night.

"Thanks again for the drink," Mia said, her voice barely audible.

He nodded, but he was already invisible to her again as she turned and left, letting in a whoosh of the freezing winter air.

Padraig remained where he was for about a minute before walking out from behind the counter and over to Finn.

"Hey, cuz. Can you do me a favor? Cover the bar for a few minutes? I need to take care of something real quick."

Finn rose without hesitation. "Sure thing." He jerked his head toward the counter. "Come on, guys. Grab your drinks and we'll carry on over there."

Padraig rushed toward the front door, slightly annoyed when Finn called out to him.

"You're going outside?" Finn asked.

"Yeah."

Finn gestured to his coat, still lying in the booth he'd just vacated. "Wear my coat or you'll freeze your nuts off."

Padraig grabbed the jacket, pulling it on as he rushed outside. The cold air hit him like a brick to the face, his chest ironically burning from the chill as he breathed.

15

He thought he'd have to race to catch up with Mia, so he was surprised to discover she was still standing just outside the pub.

"Mia," he said, stepping next to her.

She glanced at him with a dull expression.

"Kind of cold to hang about too long."

It occurred to him that she hadn't even noticed the temperature until he mentioned it.

"It doesn't bother me."

He gave her an incredulous look. "Pretty sure you're the only person in Baltimore who feels that way. Is this Chicago conditioning?"

She shook her head, not offering anything more. Her eyes drifted away from him, and he recalled why he'd chased after her.

"Mia," he said firmly, waiting until she faced him. "What's wrong?"

She pressed her eyes closed tightly, but she was too late to trap in the tears that fell down her cheeks.

Padraig acted on instinct, reaching out and tugging her toward him for a hug. She accepted his embrace without hesitance, no longer bothering to hide her crying.

He held her, not sure what else to do. He was no stranger to crying. His time at the pub ensured he'd consoled more than his fair share of women—and sometimes even men—who'd consumed too much alcohol and sobbed out their woes.

This time felt different. For one thing, Mia wasn't drunk. And for another, her pain seemed bone-deep, more grief than lost love or job.

"It's okay," he soothed. "It's okay."

She pulled away at the sound of his voice and for the first time since she'd walked into the pub, he felt like she was finally seeing him.

"Padraig?" she shuddered. "I…I'm…" Her words came out in starts and stops as she struggled to catch her breath between barely contained sobs. "S-sorry."

He started to reach for her again, wishing there was some way he could console her. He didn't know her well, but he hated seeing her in such intense pain. She took another step away, shaking her head.

"I'm so sorry," she repeated. "I didn't mean to…fall apart…" Even as she spoke, the tears continued. She was losing the fight to regain control of her emotions.

"It's okay, Mia. I'm here. I'd like to help if you'd let me."

She pressed a gloved hand to her trembling lips. "You can't. No one…"

"What is it? Please. Tell me what happened."

Mia looked down, sucking in several deep breaths as she tried once more to stop crying.

"Did someone die? Someone you love?" he asked gently.

He regretted the question the moment she crumpled. Completely.

She fell into his arms and sobbed, her agony almost palpable.

Padraig held her for several minutes, just let all the pain find its way to the surface and out. He rocked her slowly in his arms as he tried to recall what he knew about Mia Curtis.

Precious little, he realized.

She was from Chicago. She'd moved to Baltimore for a job opportunity. She lived alone. Knew no one in the city, and she rooted for the Blackhawks and the Bears.

That was it.

"Is there someone you'd like me to call?" he asked as her crying began to slow and quiet.

She shook her head.

"A friend from work? Family?"

"No," she whispered. "There's no one."

Her answer gutted him almost as much as her crying. He'd grown up with an abundance of family and friends. Hell, half the time he joked he had too many damn relatives.

To consider that she was in so much distress with no one to call for help was upsetting. It bothered him deeply.

While he didn't know her well, he knew people. And his gut told him she was a genuinely nice person. So why was a nice person living alone with no friends and crying her heart out to a stranger because she had no one else to turn to?

For a moment, he considered calling one of his female cousins, perhaps Yvonne or Sunnie, to talk to Mia. Maybe she couldn't confide whatever was wrong to him because he was a man.

Before he could make the offer, she seemed to have found her strength at last.

She stood straighter, finally managing to reclaim her voice. "I didn't mean to fall apart like that. I realize I must look like an insane person."

"No. You look like someone who needs a friend."

"It's why I came to the pub," she admitted. "I got some..." She paused, and he realized she was struggling to pick her words. "Bad news today. I was almost back to my apartment when I turned and came to the bar instead. I thought maybe it would help to be around people."

Padraig reached over and rubbed a thumb over the tracks of her tears. He forced a grin and a lighthearted voice, desperate to find some way to make her smile. "Looks like it worked."

She laughed at his joke. It was just one quick burst of humor before she sobered up again, but it pleased him. Made him determined to produce a longer smile, a louder laugh the next time.

"Yeah. Worked wonders." She glanced toward the bar. "I didn't mean to keep you away from the pub so long." She shivered, the cold finally penetrating. "Or out in this freezing air. I should let you—"

"Want to grab a cup of coffee from the Daily Grind?" he asked, pointing down the block toward the coffee shop.

"What about the bar?"

Padraig reached into the back pocket of his jeans and pulled out his cell. "My cousin is covering for me. I'm sure he won't mind taking over the rest of the shift." He was pretty sure Finn *would* mind, but he'd find a way to make it up to him. "Let me just text him and we'll be on our way."

She looked across the street at her apartment building. Padraig was afraid she'd insist on going home. He wasn't comfortable leaving her alone. At least not until he found out what was wrong. Mia was in serious pain, and even if she was used to dealing with things on her own, that wasn't the Collins way. It simply wasn't in him to leave her alone and hurting.

He was relieved when she nodded, waiting patiently as he sent his pleading text to Finn.

Padraig didn't bother to wait for a reply. Instead, he reached out, grasped her hand, and the two of them walked to the coffee shop.

His phone beeped just as they crossed the threshold.

All Finn said was, *You owe me.*

They both ordered tall Americanas, then claimed a small table in a quiet corner. This place—like Pat's

Pub—was nearly empty. Didn't look like hot drinks were faring any better than alcohol in this weather.

Mia wrapped her hands around her cup, seeking the warmth it provided, and he followed suit.

They sat in silence for a few moments.

"I realize I'm a stranger to you," he said at last.

Before he could continue, she interrupted. "Not really. I mean, I know we don't talk a lot, but I'm in the pub enough that I've formed a pretty good picture of who you are."

His curiosity was piqued. "Oh yeah? Like what?"

"You've got a good sense of humor. You're obsessed with sports and probably skirting a line in terms of gambling addiction."

He laughed. "That vice is pretty common in my family."

She smiled. "I like your family. Like that so many of you work together in Pat's Pub. You're all really nice to each other. I mean, it feels like you actually like each other."

He tilted his head. "We're family. Of course we like each other. Actually, we love each other."

"I like that you don't have a clue how unique your family is. None of you seem to realize that."

Her comment gave him his first real insight into her own family situation. "You're not close to your family?"

"No," she admitted. "Unlike you, my family tree is a lot smaller. Me and my mom. And we've been estranged since I was seventeen."

Padraig didn't have a clue how old she was, but he figured it was rude to ask. "I'm sorry to hear that."

"Don't be. My life got a lot simpler when I stopped trying to make my mother into something she wasn't."

"No dad?"

"Sperm donor. Mom got pregnant in high school. Guy basically rejected her...and me. Pretty sure my mom would have had an abortion or given me up for adoption if not for my grandma."

Mia smiled when she mentioned her grandmother, and Padraig felt a strange sense of relief. He could tell from her expression that mercifully there'd been at least one person in Mia's past who had wanted her, loved her.

"Mom and I lived with my grandma until I was eleven. Grandma took care of me while my mom finished high school and then went to work. Grandma was the most amazing person I've ever known. She used to call me Tilly Mint."

"What's that stand for?"

Mia shrugged. "No idea. Just a silly nickname, I guess. But I was always sorry I never asked her."

"What happened when you were eleven?" He regretted his question. Whatever had been upsetting Mia before seemed to return.

"C-cancer," she said, stumbling over the word. She looked down at her coffee, her eyes returning to that faraway look that told Padraig he'd lost her again.

"Mia," he said, reaching over and giving one of her hands a light squeeze. "That must have been hard on you."

She nodded. "My mom had basically washed her hands of me after I was born, so without Grandma, she was forced into a parenting position she didn't want. And I didn't help much. I missed Grandma so much and I resented my mom. I mean, she'd never made any secret of her feelings for me, so when she tried to tell me what to do, I got angry, rebellious. We butted heads nonstop until halfway through my senior year, when I moved out. I had a friend whose parents were cool with me sleeping on the couch in their basement until graduation. I worked two jobs to try to pay my own way."

Padraig tried to imagine how frightening it must have been to have no support system at such a young age. "You haven't talked to your mom since then?"

"No. I ran into her once when I was twenty. I was working the checkout line at the grocery store and Mom got in my line. I'm sure she wouldn't have if she'd looked up and realized it was me working the register. I rang up the groceries at record speed, she paid, and that was it. As far as I know, she never darkened the door of that store again."

"She didn't even ask how you were?"

Mia shook her head. "No. But in all fairness, I didn't ask about her, either."

Padraig made a mental note to call his mom first thing in the morning to tell her he loved her.

Mia took a sip of her coffee and he followed suit.

"I hope you won't think I'm a stalker, but I like coming into the pub to watch you and your family interact. I had a blast last month, sitting at the bar to watch that *February Stars* competition with everyone. It was fun."

Padraig felt guilty for not even realizing she'd been there. Of course, in his defense, the bar had been packed on competition nights. They'd streamed the show live on all the televisions, as family members and patrons placed wagers on who would win the contest. Business had been really terrific that month, which made the sudden slowdown in March all the more brutal. There had been too many nights the past few weeks that he'd been bored out of his mind, certain it would be more exciting to watch paint dry.

"*February Stars* was a fun contest," he said.

"I was glad when Hunter ultimately won. He was my favorite the whole time."

22

"Yeah. He was my cousin Ailis's favorite too." Ailis and Hunter had fallen in love during the contest and were in the midst of planning a future together. She was the second of Padraig's pile of cousins to be bitten by the love bug. His oldest cousin, Caitlyn, was currently head over heels with Lucas Whiting, the richest guy in Baltimore.

"Let me guess. You were a Rory fan?"

Padraig grinned. "Not sure there were too many guys who weren't in her camp. My brother is half in love with her, even though he won't admit it. And there's no denying her voice is out of this world."

"Doesn't hurt that she's gorgeous, either," Mia teased.

"She is?" he joked. "I hadn't noticed."

Mia rolled her eyes. "So Ailis and Hunter…they're a thing now?"

Padraig nodded. "Yep. They're a thing." He figured he knew the answer to his next question, but he asked it anyway. "What about you? You have a thing for anybody?"

"No. I haven't dated anyone since moving to Baltimore."

"And in Chicago?"

She shrugged. "I had a couple boyfriends but nothing super serious. You may find this hard to believe, but I have trust issues. Can't begin to understand where those stem from."

He chuckled at her sarcasm. "Me, either," he said, piling on. "I mean, your upbringing was so stellar."

"Right?" she said, eyes wide with feigned agreement. "What about you? Anything serious between you and the woman you asked out over the phone last week?"

He gave her a curious glance, and she flushed a little.

"Sorry," she muttered. "I wasn't really eavesdropping. It's just, when you eat alone, it's hard not to hear the conversations going on around you."

"The woman's name is Brooke and we've gone out a few times. She's really nice."

"Cool."

"You know, I have some single cousins and a bachelor brother if you want me to set you up." As soon as he made the offer, Padraig began trying to decide which relative he'd choose for the blind date. In truth, he suspected all his cousins and Colm would enjoy dating Mia.

She shook her head, the sadness returning to her face. "No. That's okay. I don't think…it's not a good time for…" Her voice grew thicker with each word, until she finally gave up speaking.

"Every time I think I've distracted you, it comes back, doesn't it?"

Mia closed her eyes wearily. "It keeps sneaking up on me, blindsiding me. I forget for a minute or two and then boom. I'm body-slammed back down to the ground."

He hated to press her, to keep questioning. It was obvious she didn't want to talk about whatever it was that was attacking her.

"Want me to keep distracting you?"

She smiled. "I'd like that."

"So tell me about your job."

Chapter Two

Padraig took another sip of coffee as Mia explained how she'd managed to escape a long line of dead-end jobs by taking business courses online. He was impressed by her intelligence and drive. Unhappy and barely getting by while working several minimum-wage jobs at the same time, she'd added even more to her plate in order to get a degree.

Her hard work had paid off, and she'd landed a job as manager in an office supply store. The owner, Phyllis, had apparently been so impressed with Mia's work ethic that she'd put her in charge of opening a new store here in Baltimore. Four months in, and she'd already managed to stock the shelves and hire the staff.

"The grand opening is next week, but now…"

Padraig was becoming accustomed to her pregnant pauses. "Now?" he prodded, wishing she would confide what was wrong.

"Now…I'm not sure what will happen."

"Mia," he started.

"I want to tell you, Padraig. I swear to God, I do. It's just…I can't find a way to say the words. They're stuck."

Now he understood. It wasn't that she didn't want to confide in him. It was that she couldn't.

Once again, his mind whirled over what could be so bad that she couldn't speak the words. Given her concern about work, he thought he'd figured it out.

She'd spoken as fondly of Phyllis as she had her grandmother. Had the woman passed away? Had she lost yet another person she cared about and now she was in fear of losing her job?

"So what do you think about Baltimore?" he asked, deciding he'd give her more time to sort out her emotions. Pushing her wouldn't help.

"I love it here. I was nervous when Phyllis asked me to move halfway across the country, but then, it felt like a chance to grab a fresh start."

"Did you need a fresh start?"

She lifted one shoulder. "Isn't that what life is? One more fresh start, one more clean break. If you want to get super deep, you could say every single morning is the equivalent of starting over."

"You're right. It is."

"I like the energy in this city. Don't get me wrong. There was plenty to love about Chicago too, but there's something about this place. The peacefulness of walking by the water, the Inner Harbor, the quaintness of the cobblestone streets, the unique buildings and abundance of Irish pubs."

He laughed. "Are you saying my family's business is a Baltimore cliché?"

He was growing quite fond of her sarcastic humor. "Not at all. Actually, Pat's Pub has become my favorite place in the city. I can sit at the counter and not feel quite so alone."

"I'm glad. And you're right. It is a pretty special place."

"Has it always belonged to your family?"

Padraig shook his head. "My Pop Pop took the business over from an old family friend back in the sixties. Immigrated to America from Ireland with his wife, my grandma Sunday."

"Your Pop Pop is the older gentleman who sits in the center stool at the bar sometimes, right?"

"Yeah. Guy is a very spry ninety-two. He served drinks at the pub full time with my dad until he was in his mid-seventies."

"Seems like a cool guy."

"The coolest." Padraig loved talking about his family, especially his grandfather. He was proud of his heritage. "Can't imagine it was easy for him and Grandma Sunday, working the pub while raising seven kids."

Mia's eyes widened. "Seven? I knew it was a pretty big family, but I had no idea. To tell you the truth, I've sort of made it a game to figure out who's who in the Collins tribe. I figured out who your grandfather was, but where's your grandma?"

"She died a long time ago." He started to add the word "cancer" but stopped himself. He recalled how she'd stumbled over the word when talking about her own grandmother. Padraig had started to compile a list of triggers when it came to her sadness. "My aunt Keira is the oldest of the seven kids."

"So give me the abbreviated family tree. I want to see how much I've gotten right."

Padraig laughed. "Even abbreviated, this could take a while. How long do you have?"

"Six months."

He laughed at her joke even though he didn't get it, and he noticed she didn't crack a smile. "That should be enough time. My aunt Keira married a man named Will, and they have two kids, Caitlyn and Lochlan."

"Caitlyn is the one who's dating Lucas Whiting, right?"

"She hates that everyone in the world knows that."

27

Mia took a quick sip of her coffee. "There's no way the world *isn't* going to know that. The guy is a billionaire and Baltimore hottie. Hard to open the newspaper and not see their picture coming and going from some ritzy fundraiser."

"True."

"So who came next?"

"Teagan."

"I still can't believe Teagan Collins and Sky Mitchell are your aunt and uncle. That must be amazing. Have you gone to a lot of their shows?"

"Do their impromptu concerts at the pub count?"

She considered that, and then nodded. "Yeah. I think those might count twice. It's like getting your own private show."

"Never thought of it that way, but I guess you're right."

"Ailis is their daughter, right? The lucky girl who's dating Hunter."

Padraig rolled his eyes. "I knew it. You've got the hots for Hunter."

"Every woman has the hots for Hunter Maxwell, now that he's won *February Stars* and is destined for stardom."

"Good point. Ailis has a sister named Fiona. She's writes for television and lives in L.A."

"That sounds like an awesome job. Who's next?"

"My dad. He and my mom had me and Colm."

"The twin brother who looks just like you. I have to admit, it freaked me out the first time I saw you two together. I didn't know he existed and then boom, suddenly there are two of you."

Padraig laughed. "We get that a lot. Used to switch places to try to fool friends and teachers at school."

"Did it work?"

"More times than it didn't. Of course, we'd always get in trouble for it later at home. Our parents were never fooled."

Mia pushed her almost-empty cup away.

"Want another one?" he asked.

"No. I'm afraid the caffeine from that one will keep me up all night as it is. Must be cool having a twin. Or even just a sibling. I would have loved to have a brother or sister."

"Colm is awesome. My best friend."

She smiled. "You're so lucky."

"I know."

"And after your dad came...?" she prompted.

"His twin brother, Killian."

"Are they identical too?"

Padraig nodded. "Yep. Killian is married to Justin and Lily." He paused, studying her face as she absorbed that information.

"Both of them? Is that legal?"

"Lily is married to Killian, according to the state of Maryland, but in their hearts and minds, it's the three of them. Always has been, apparently. They all went to high school together."

Padraig didn't go on with his family history, waiting instead to see if Mia would make a disparaging comment about the threesome. He'd certainly heard enough nasty things muttered under the breaths of others. In his mind, the easiest way to learn someone's true nature was to see how they responded. He had no respect for people who passed judgment on three people who had fallen in love with each other.

"I think that's sweet. Do they have any kids?"

He released the breath he'd been holding. "Just one. Fergus."

She counted on her fingers, doing the math. "Okay, so that's four kids. Three more to go."

"Next is Ewan, who runs Sunday's Side with Aunt Keira. He's married to Natalie and they have one daughter, Yvonne." One of the two cousins he'd considered calling earlier when Mia fell apart. "She lives upstairs in the Collins Dorm, along with…well…a bunch of us."

Mia laughed. "Now *that* part I had figured out. I heard your aunt Riley, the cook, call it that, and given all the cousins I've seen going in and out of the door that leads upstairs, I figured there must be a big-ass apartment up there."

"Touché. Extra credit for figuring out the living arrangements. Speaking of Aunt Riley, she and my uncle Aaron have three kids, Sunnie, Darcy and Finn."

"Finn is the cousin who's covering your shift tonight?"

"Yeah."

"That was nice of him."

"He's a good guy."

"So is there a last, but not least?" she asked.

"The youngest is Sean. He's married to Lauren and Chad, and they have one son, Oliver."

"You might have the most interesting family in the history of the world."

He could tell from her expression she meant that sincerely and kindly. "They're the best. How much of that had you figured out?"

"Less than fifty percent. Terrible, huh?"

Padraig drained his own coffee, feeling the effects of the caffeine himself. While it was getting late, he was pumped up, energized. He liked talking to Mia, liked getting to know her. The more time he spent with her, the more he realized his first impression was right. She was a very nice person.

And pretty. He'd never really noticed her appearance prior to tonight. Never let himself dwell on her bright green eyes or strawberry-blonde hair. Even with the red-rimmed eyes left behind after her crying, she was attractive in a wholesome, clean-cut, freckle-cheeked way.

"I need to say thank you, Padraig. For tonight."

"It's nothing."

"No," she disagreed. "That's just it. It's not nothing. I…"

She'd been on the verge of revealing her pain to him. He knew it. And once again, the words got jammed up.

"Say it," he urged with a whisper. "Just say it, Mia, and I promise you, I'll help you deal with it. No matter what. Okay?"

"I'm dying."

Chapter Three

Mia wanted to suck the words back in the second she spoke them. For one thing, saying them aloud seemed to make them all the more real. And secondly, Padraig had been very kind to her tonight, and she felt incredibly guilty, dropping something like that on him without any preamble or warning.

His shell-shocked expression told her she'd handled it badly.

"Dying?" He was shaking his head, as if wondering if he'd heard her correctly.

She couldn't repeat herself. It had taken her hours to be able to say it just once. And even now, she was still struggling to believe it.

An inoperable brain tumor.

The words had been echoing over and over in her disease-riddled mind ever since Dr. Richards had pointed to the shadowy mass on the X-ray and told her what it was.

She'd gone to him because of migraines. At least, that's what she'd thought was the cause of the headaches. That or stress.

If only it had been something so simple. Something treatable.

Dr. Richards had pointed to the tumor and explained that because of the size and location, it wasn't something that could be removed. And while he offered radiation and chemotherapy as options to slow the growth, neither treatment would cure her.

Her choices had been limited to two: Accept her death sentence and try to make the most of her remaining days; or fight the ticking time bomb in her head with poisons that would ensure the few months she had left would be spent in hospitals, miserable and sick.

She'd told Dr. Richards she would consider her options, and left. Then she had walked around the hospital corridors for the better part of two hours, trying to make the words sink in.

Finally, she'd caught a cab back to her place, thinking perhaps it would be easier to come to grips with it in a familiar, comfortable environment.

She'd paid the taxi fare, looked up at the window of her apartment, then turned around and walked straight to Pat's Pub.

"Mia," Padraig prodded, pulling her out of her nightmare memories. "What do you mean, you're dying?"

"Brain tumor." Funny how those two words weren't any easier to say than "I'm dying."

Padraig shook his head again, as if denial would change the truth. That had been *her* initial response as well, and oddly, she took comfort in that shared reaction.

When Dr. Richards called her this morning, he'd urged her to bring a family member or friend with her to the appointment. That request had been a pretty major red flag. One that felt equally horrible when she'd had to acknowledge she didn't have a single person on the planet to take with her.

She wished she and Padraig had had this conversation earlier. Maybe if they'd moved toward friendship prior to tonight, she would have felt comfortable enough to ask him to go with her.

As it was, the more hours that passed, the more she realized she'd only heard about a tenth of what the doctor had said after he'd told her she was dying. She would have to get a grip at some point so she could go back with a list of questions, and a way of holding the numbness and disbelief at bay so she could absorb the information she needed.

Maybe Dr. Richards would let her record the next visit.

He'd given her brochures and suggested some websites she could use to find answers as well. They were tucked in her purse and, even now, she couldn't make herself pull them out to look over.

"You *can't* be dying, Mia. You're young. You're healthy."

She'd said the same things. Assured Dr. Richards that apart from the headaches, she felt great. "Apparently, tumors don't just seek out old people."

"They can operate. Take it out." Padraig was grasping for all the same branches she'd reached for.

"Inoperable. It's in a bad place."

"Drugs. Chemo."

She shook her head. "Wouldn't help."

"Fuck this!" Padraig's voice grew louder, and she soaked up his outrage on her behalf like cooling aloe on scorched summer skin. "We're getting a second opinion."

She laughed. She didn't mean to. What he said wasn't funny. Rather, it was probably the nicest thing anyone had ever said to her. *We're* getting a second opinion. Not *you*. He'd joined her team, tied himself to her. The girl who had only ever been a singular pronoun was suddenly part of a plural.

"I mean it," Padraig said, unsmiling. "We're not taking one quack's word for this. He's wrong."

"We?" she asked, trying—but failing—to hide her grin.

"Of course, *we*. Jesus. I'm not a heartless prick. You're new to the city with no family or friends to help you through this. Do you seriously think I'm going to say, 'Hey, good talk,' and walk away from you?"

"Tonight is the first time we've ever really spoken. How would I know what to think?"

He sighed. "You're right. I get it. Up until a couple of hours ago, we probably couldn't have even said we were acquaintances. But now..."

Padraig reached over and took her hand. It wasn't the first time he'd comforted her with that small touch, but now that he knew—knew and wanted to help her—it sent a wave of...

Of what? She tried to latch onto an emotion, but couldn't. She'd been through the wringer today, waffling between numbness, devastation and merciful distraction.

"Now we're friends." Padraig didn't release her hand this time after a quick, reassuring squeeze.

Instead, he held tight, and she realized what she was feeling was hope.

It was a ridiculous response, considering there was none. But the feeling was there, and as long as Padraig held her hand, it remained stubbornly ensconced.

"I like the sound of friends."

His face was still somber, and she hated that she'd wiped away the easy smile he'd worn most of the evening. "What did the doctor say? Exactly?" he asked.

She shrugged. "I lost track of most of the words after 'inoperable brain tumor' and 'six months to live'."

35

"Six months?" he repeated, and she remembered her tasteless joke earlier. The words had fallen out without thought, bitterly, though Padraig hadn't caught the tone behind them.

"I shouldn't have said that before. I—"

"It's okay, Mia. My mom is a nurse. If you'd allow it, I think she should go with you to your next appointment. She'll understand what's being said and can ask questions, clarify things. I also want to get her suggestions about who you should see for a second opinion. She's been a nurse in Baltimore forever. I swear it seems like she knows every doctor in the state."

Mia felt another tear slide down her cheek. She'd foolishly thought she had sobbed all of those out against Padraig's chest outside. His offer was the answer to a prayer, and she was touched. "I'd like that a lot."

They were interrupted when the clerk walked over to their table. "Getting ready to close up."

Padraig and Mia both stood and put their coats back on. Mia tried to push down the panic rising in her chest. As long as she was with Padraig, she could keep a grip on herself. The idea of climbing the stairs to her apartment and sitting alone with nothing but her fear and her sadness, terrified her.

But she couldn't ask Padraig to keep hanging around. It was eleven o'clock and he'd already blown off a night's work to comfort her. While he'd offered his friendship and support, that didn't mean he would stay with her 24/7 to keep her from losing her shit every time she recalled the fact that she was dying.

She sucked in a deep breath that sounded like a sob as they stepped out on the street. Padraig stopped and looked at her.

"Where to?" he asked.

"Don't you want to go home? It's late. I've already monopolized your entire night."

He studied her face. She didn't have the ability to feign a strength she didn't feel. "It's still early. Where do you want to go? Back to the pub?"

She shook her head. While the place hadn't been exactly buzzing tonight, she really wasn't sure she could hold herself together in front of people. Now that Padraig knew what was going on, she felt the need to talk. She'd been trying to reason it out in her head, but she couldn't. She had a million things she wanted to say, and he was the only person around to listen.

"My apartment is just a block away. I have some wine. Maybe if I drink enough of it, I can pass out instead of crying myself to sleep."

Padraig tucked his arm around her shoulders, turning them toward her place. "Wine sounds good. You sure you trust me not to take advantage of you?"

She could tell he was trying to lighten the moment. Truth was, she'd watched him at the pub enough to know Padraig Collins was a stand-up guy. A gentleman.

And as reassuring as that was, there was a part of her that actually wouldn't have minded the "taking advantage" part, simply because it would involve touching, feeling, and not sleeping alone.

For a woman who had spent the better part of her life completely alone and not being bothered by it, she couldn't seem to shake the loneliness that had crashed in on her since the doctor's diagnosis.

"I trust you," she said, and they walked the rest of the way to her place in silence.

They climbed the stairs to her second-floor apartment and she unlocked the door, inviting him in. She tossed her coat on a chair near the door, then took his and laid it over hers. She gestured to the couch.

"Have a seat and I'll pour us both a glass. It's cab sav. Is that okay?"

"Sounds great."

She walked to the kitchen and poured two glasses of wine. Her hand trembled slightly as she did so, and she spilled a few drops on the counter. She wiped it up and took a deep breath, trying to steady herself. She couldn't keep falling apart in front of Padraig or he would go running for the hills.

Mia picked up the glasses and returned to the living room. Padraig rose from the couch, taking the wine she offered. He lightly tapped his glass against hers before sitting back down. She claimed the opposite end of the couch and they each took a sip.

"When is your next doctor's appointment?" he asked as he set his glass on a coaster on the coffee table.

"Tuesday. I understand if your mom can't make that work. It's short notice."

"She'll make it work," he replied with complete confidence. "I know she'll want to be there once I explain the situation."

Mia wasn't sure which situation he was referring to. Her health or her motherless state. But both worked so she rolled with it. Having someone with a medical background go with her really would help. Dr. Richards had said too many things she didn't understand today. Not that she'd been firing on all cylinders.

Yet another tear rolled down her cheek and she batted it away quickly. Unfortunately, not before Padraig saw it.

"I'm sorry," she whispered. "I don't mean to keep crying. I swear I'm trying to keep it together."

Padraig scooted closer, near enough that he could take the wineglass from her hand and set it next to his. Then he clasped hands with her. She'd never realized such a sweet, innocent gesture as holding hands could be so comforting.

"I think you're entitled to those tears, Mia. I'm not sure how you're holding it together as well as you are. If I'd gotten news like yours, I'd be curled up in a fetal position in some dark corner of my bedroom."

She grinned, even though she doubted his assertion. Padraig seemed like the type of man who could face anything that came his way. But she appreciated his attempts at bolstering her up.

"I just..." She paused as she considered all the things she'd been thinking of when she was supposed to be listening to the doctor.

"You just what?"

"I thought I had time. Time to do so many things."

"Like what?"

The list flowed easily, because it wasn't a new one. "Like get married. Have a family of my own. Adopt a really badly behaved dog. Sing karaoke loud and off-key. Travel to Paris and Harry Potter World. Dance my ass off in some nightclub and see the ocean...just once. And I really—" Her voice broke. "God, I really want to eat chocolate cake with my bare freaking hands on my next birthday. And I want to eat the whole cake myself. I don't want to share it."

"When's your birthday?"

"October second. Close, but no cigar." It was an attempt at a joke. It fell short.

"How old will you be?"

"Twenty-seven. Guess if there's a bright side, I don't have to worry about hitting the dreaded thirty."

"You don't have to do that on my account."

"Do what?" she asked.

"Joke around about something that's not funny just to lighten the mood. You don't have to be afraid of being real in front of me. I think if there was ever a time to drop all pretense and be yourself, it's now."

She sighed. "Yeah. You're right."

"So tell me who you are. Three things—your best qualities."

She grinned. "Only three?"

Padraig laughed. "I like a woman who knows her own worth. So what are they?"

"It's hard to rattle off a list like that without sounding cocky."

Padraig shook his head. "I disagree. Society always seems to focus too much on the negative. Probably be a better world if we gave people more credit for the things they do well, do right."

"Fine. We'll take turns. I'm a hard worker." She didn't add that she'd had to be to survive. "What about you?"

"I'm a good listener."

She nodded. "Yeah, you are. I'm an amazing cook."

"Really?" he said. "I think I'm going to need you to prove that to me sometime."

Mia picked up her wine with her free hand. She didn't want to let go of the link between her and Padraig. She took a drink, liking the way the red wine warmed her from the inside out as it slid down her throat. "Your turn," she prompted.

"I have a great sense of humor."

"Oh yeah?" she teased. "You really want to go with great? Not just so-so or fair? Because you need to keep in mind, I've heard some of those corny jokes you tell at the bar. 'Great' seems to be reaching."

Padraig barked out a loud laugh, and she realized he never held back when he found something funny. He laughed with his whole body. "Damn. I know I told you to be real, but maybe we should reconsider that. You need to dial it back a notch, woman."

Mia giggled.

"You've really never seen the ocean?" he asked.

She shook her head. "Born and raised in Chicago, as you know. Solid Midwest. Never any money for a big trip like that. Then I moved here in November. Planned to drive to the coast this summer."

"It's definitely worth the trip."

She sighed, wondering if she'd be well enough come summer. "Yeah," she replied, though her tone reflected her disbelief.

He squeezed her hand. "You're going to see your next birthday, Mia. I'm sure of it."

That damn hope that he kept poking and prodding reared its head again and for three whole seconds, she believed he was right. However, like every other emotion she'd experienced that day, it was brief. Fleeting.

"I always felt like my list was life goals. Now…now they seem more like a list of regrets."

Padraig's expression sobered. "Don't give up, Mia."

"I'm scared," she whispered, admitting the one thing she hadn't been able to shake all day. The excruciating, bone-shaking terror.

"I know." Padraig wrapped his arm around her shoulders and for the second time that night, he let her cry out all her fear, all her agony, against his strong chest.

Rather than try to stop—as she had out on the street—this time, she just let go. Let it all come out in a mess of tears, loud sobs, and curses.

"It's not fair. It's not fucking fair!"

Padraig held her through it all. Not letting go even when the storm calmed and the numbness returned.

41

Mia closed her eyes, exhausted, Padraig's words the last thing she heard before she fell sleep.

"I'm here now. It'll be okay."

Chapter Four

March 29

Padraig stood at the railing, looking out across the water. He'd remained at Mia's until just after dawn, holding her as she slept. Then he'd laid her down on the couch, tucked her in and left a note with his phone number on it, asking her to call him later with the details about her doctor's appointment.

The wind had died down a bit from the previous night, but not even the bright sun could penetrate the chill in the air. After leaving Mia's apartment, he'd started to head home. However, he walked right by the pub, too keyed up and anxious to consider sleeping. Padraig did his best thinking while walking, so he'd spent the better part of three hours, zigzagging his way all over Baltimore as he'd tried to gather his thoughts, tried to find logic in something that didn't make sense.

Twenty-six-year-old women didn't die.

And while he knew that wasn't true, he knew it should be.

Padraig was perfectly aware of the old adage that life wasn't fair, but sometimes it went beyond unfair and straight to complete and utter shit.

He'd spent exactly twelve hours with Mia. Just twelve. And when he thought about her dying, it felt as if he'd been kicked in the gut. Probably because he wasn't that much older than her, and he definitely wasn't ready to die.

Like her, he had a list of things he wanted to do, and his list mirrored quite a bit of hers. Marriage, family, pets, travel. Even with the simpler things that were easier to accomplish. Mia wanted to dance in a club. He wanted to run in a marathon.

She wanted to see her next birthday, and now...he wanted to *see her* on that birthday. To watch her blow out the candles and plow through the cake, using nothing but her hands.

When he considered that, his path seemed very clear. Very straightforward.

And the idea that had kept him out of bed, walking the streets 'til dawn, took root. Held fast.

"Guess that settles that," he murmured to the water, the anxiety he'd been suffering all night suddenly vanishing.

Despite his lack of sleep, there was a spring in his step now as he walked back to the pub. He'd made up his mind.

Padraig hadn't made it a few feet inside before he spotted his dad behind the bar, unpacking a box of liquor, restocking the shelves.

Dad turned, giving him a quick up and down. "Out early or in late?"

"The latter," he admitted as he sank down on a stool across the counter from his father.

"Ewan said Finn finished up your shift for you last night. Out with that new girl? What's her name? Brooke?"

Padraig shook his head. "No. Not Brooke." His father's question reminded him that he needed to add one more thing to his to-do list. Call Brooke and break things off.

His response caught his dad's attention. "No? Thought you liked Brooke."

"I did. Do," he corrected. "But it's not going to work out between us."

"Why not?"

"Because..." Padraig took a deep breath. "I'm marrying someone else."

Dad frowned. "Who?"

"Mia Curtis."

"Who the hell is that?"

Padraig had anticipated the shocked response. After all, he'd just announced he was marrying a complete stranger. Regardless, Padraig's mind was made up, and he wouldn't be swayed. Which meant he needed to make his family understand.

"She's a regular here at the pub. Moved to Baltimore about four months ago. Usually sits there." Padraig pointed to Mia's usual stool. "Reddish-blonde hair, green eyes, pretty, quiet. Roots for Chicago."

Padraig should have led with the sports information. Dad was pretty good with names and faces, but he was Einstein when it came to remembering who everyone who'd ever darkened the door of the pub rooted for.

"I know who you mean. Didn't realize the two of you were dating," his dad said, obviously still confused.

"We aren't."

Dad put down the bottle of bourbon he'd been holding throughout their conversation and rested his palms on the low counter behind the bar. "Maybe we should take this from the top, because I'm missing a few hundred pieces. You're marrying a stranger—"

"Mia," Padraig added.

"You're marrying this woman you barely know, whose name is Mia, because..." Dad paused, waiting for Padraig to fill in the blank.

"Because she's dying."

Dad never missed a beat. "Keep going."

"She came into the bar last night, and I could tell something was wrong. She was visibly upset when she left, so I asked Finn to cover for me while I followed her to make sure she was okay."

Dad nodded approvingly.

"She broke down just outside. The wind was brutal last night, so we walked to the Daily Grind, talked for a while. About everything—our families, our jobs. And then, she dropped the bomb. Said she has an inoperable brain tumor. Six months to live."

"Jesus," Dad muttered. "Poor little thing."

"I walked her back to her place and we talked some more." Padraig recalled his promise to Mia. "I was hoping Mom would go with her to her next doctor's appointment. She went alone yesterday, and I'm not sure she heard much of anything else the guy said after he told her she was dying. Figure Mom might know what questions to ask, and suggest another doctor so Mia can get a second opinion."

Dad rubbed his chin. "I'm sure your mom would be happy to. In fact, when you tell her what you're telling me, I suspect she'll insist on it."

"She's got nobody, Dad," Padraig said at last. It was that part that bothered him the most. If, God forbid, he'd received the same diagnosis, Padraig would have been surrounded by no less than fifty friends and relatives, all ready to support him, care for him. "She's new in town and estranged from her mother, who sounds like a pretty nasty person."

"Paddy. You've got a heart as big as California. You always have. But, son, you can support this woman as her friend. You don't have to marry her."

"She, uh...she had a list of things she always thought she'd do before she died. First thing on it was to get married."

"Did she ask you to marry her?" Dad asked.

Padraig shook his head. "God no. She doesn't even know I'm thinking about it. Knowing her, she'll turn me down flat. I'm going to have to take some time, help her work her way through the rest of her list and then, hopefully, I'll be able to convince her."

"Convince who?"

Padraig turned, surprised to see Pop Pop standing behind him.

"You're here early."

"Breakfast special is the Full Irish. You know I never miss that." Pop Pop also never missed gossip. He'd arrived just in time to catch the very end of their conversation, and his curiosity was piqued. "So who are you convincing? And what are you trying to get them to do?"

"I'm going to ask Mia Curtis to marry me."

Dad sighed and muttered something incoherent.

"I thought your girlfriend's name was Brooke?" Pop Pop replied.

Padraig wondered if it wouldn't be easier to call a family meeting and give them this news all together.

"Brooke isn't my girlfriend. We've only gone out on a handful of dates." Padraig looked from his grandfather to his dad. He'd spent his entire life emulating these men, trying to be like them. He didn't doubt for a second they would understand why he wanted to marry Mia. He just needed to do a lot better job explaining it.

"Mia has an inoperable brain tumor, Pop Pop. The doctor has given her six months to live."

"Oh my." Pop Pop shook his head sadly. "She's the little redhead who holds up the end of the bar every now and again, right?"

Padraig nodded. There was very little his Pop Pop didn't notice.

"So young," Pop Pop said with a sigh.

Dad ran his hand through his hair, giving away the stress Padraig's announcement was causing him. "Apparently, she and Padraig spent a great deal of time together last night, and now—"

"I want to help her live the life she imagined for herself when she thought she had decades instead of months. She has a list. A bucket list, I guess you could say."

Pop Pop was quiet for a moment, so Padraig followed suit, giving the older man time to think.

"Are you in love with this woman?" Pop Pop asked.

Padraig shook his head. "No. But I like her. A lot. She's nice and funny and stronger than she realizes. She doesn't deserve what she's been given."

"You like her," Pop Pop said, looking at him closely.

Padraig could only begin to imagine what he must look like. He'd been up all night, his eyes felt dry and scratchy from the lack of sleep. Plus, he'd spent the last few hours outside in the freezing cold. His lips were chapped, his cheeks windburned, and his hair felt frozen to his scalp.

"Death is a hard thing. I suspect she could use a friend." Pop Pop smiled at him.

"He's not talking about being her friend, Pop," Tris corrected.

"No, you're right. He wants to marry her."

Want seemed like the wrong word for a second or two. Then Padraig realized it wasn't. He *did* want to marry her. "Yeah. I do. I really do."

Pop Pop's grin grew, and Padraig got the feeling he'd heard more in his response than what he'd actually said. "So marry her."

"Pop—" Dad said, but Pop Pop raised his hand to cut him off.

"You disagree?" Pop Pop asked. "Think about it. Think about what your son is proposing to do. He wants to make a dying woman's dreams come true. He wants to ensure she doesn't die alone. Padraig plans to fill her last months with happiness, rather than sadness. If you're unhappy with his decision, then maybe you should have raised him to be more selfish, less empathetic and less kind."

Dad closed his mouth. It was damn hard to win an argument with Patrick Collins.

Padraig wasn't trying to win anything, but Pop Pop's words still resonated with him, gave him too many things to think about. Things his exhausted mind and impulsive nature hadn't really considered.

Satisfied that the matter was closed, Pop Pop turned back to Padraig. "How many things on her list are achievable in the time that's left?"

Padraig had given her list a great deal of thought this morning during his walk around the city. "All of them."

Pop Pop smiled. "Good. A person should never leave this life with regrets. So, what do you need from the family?"

Padraig knew the answer to that. "Help convincing her to let me work through the list with her. I'm basically a stranger, so I sort of need you all to help me prove to her that I'm not a lunatic."

"You're doing a pretty good impersonation of one," Dad muttered.

Pop Pop waved his hand as if Padraig's concern was inconsequential. "You're a charming, good-looking guy, Paddy. It won't be a problem. Besides, you've got a whole arsenal of relatives ready to back you up. Although, on second thought, I suspect you'll only need Riley. She can be very persuasive."

Dad shook his head. "Christ, Pop. I'm putting my foot down there. The poor woman is sick. We're not siccing Riley on her unless we need to. She's the last resort."

"Here's what you'll do." Pop Pop began detailing Padraig's plan of attack as more and more family members made their way over to the bar, adding their own ideas of how Padraig could convince Mia Curtis to spend her last six months with him.

Two hours later, he finally made it to his bed, exhausted but smiling.

***

April 1

Mia awoke to the sound of someone knocking on her door. She glanced at the clock on her DVR. It was nearly six, but for the life of her, she couldn't recall what day it was or if that six was a.m. or p.m.

Her initial doctor's appointment had been Friday afternoon, and she'd ended that day with Padraig.

Ever since Padraig had left, she'd holed herself up in her apartment. She vaguely recalled texting the assistant manager at the office, telling him she would be out on Monday. But she couldn't remember if she'd done that last night or the night before.

Waking up Saturday morning—alone—had given her too much time to think and ride on the emotional roller coaster. She was already sick of the goddamn thing. She wanted off.

Whoever was at the door knocked again. She ignored it. She hadn't showered or eaten in days. Her eyes were gritty and sore from crying so much, and she didn't feel like company.

"Mia. Open the door." It was Padraig.

Friday was the last time she'd felt like a functioning human being, and it was because of him. His kindness.

At the time, she'd needed someone to talk to, and he'd offered a shoulder to cry on. Since then, she'd given up all semblance of trying. She had pulled the shades, turned off the lights and spent three—maybe four?—days alternating between restless sleep and crying. All of it done right where Padraig had left her. On the couch.

Padraig knocked again. Louder this time. She sat up, wincing. Her neck was wicked stiff, and she could still feel the dull ache left behind from yesterday's migraine.

No. Not a migraine.

A tumor.

"Open the door, Mia, or I'm calling 9-1-1."

She slowly stood, her legs weak, wobbly.

She made herself cross the room and unlock the door, pulling it open.

Mia didn't have to check a mirror to know how bad she looked. She got a good enough sense of the damage through Padraig's frowning expression.

"Are you okay?"

She shook her head. "Nope. I'm dying."

Padraig's eyes darkened at the bitterness in her voice. "Yeah. I heard that. Thing is, I'm pretty sure you're not dying today. So go get a shower."

Now it was Mia's turn to frown. While Padraig had pledged friendship, they were nowhere near the point in their relationship where he could feel comfortable enough to tell her what to do.

"Excuse me?"

Padraig was smart enough to take heed. Rather than reply, he stepped inside and closed the door.

She'd spent the first couple of days, sitting around in a numb state of denial. This morning, she'd woken up pissed off at the world. In fact, her train was currently parked at the station of fiery outrage. Her anger was looking for an outlet, and since he was the only one here...

He glanced around the room and she followed suit. Mainly because she wasn't sure what he was going to see. The fog that had surrounded her for days was only just beginning to lift.

It was as if she'd decorated the dimly lit room to match her outfit. Tissues were strewn across every piece of furniture, along with half-empty water bottles. She'd had more success in emptying the wine bottles. There were three—that she could see—lying on their sides next to the couch. Given the fact the only visible glasses she could see were the ones she and Padraig had used Friday night, it was safe to say she'd chugged her alcohol straight from the bottle.

There was a bottle of pills on the coffee table, the contents scattered across the dusty surface. And the couch was in a state of complete disarray, covered with crumpled blankets and three pillows that looked like they'd seen twelve rounds in the ring with a heavyweight champ.

Glancing down at herself, she decided the room probably looked better. She was still in the clothes she'd been wearing on Friday. The shirt was wrinkled, stained with red wine and beyond saving. Her pants hadn't fared much better.

She ran a hand through her hair, but her fingers got stuck in the matted mess about two inches deep, and she had to give up on the quick finger brush.

"It's funny," she said, her voice sounding rough, hoarse from too many days of loud sobbing. "I used to be afraid of the dark. I'd wake up in the dead of night and panic."

"What would you do?"

"Call out for my grandma. She'd come in, and the first thing she always did was turn on the light. She'd tell me to look around, so I could see there was nothing there in the dark that wasn't there in the day. She would tell me there were no monsters lurking, not in the dark or in the light. She was wrong. There are monsters everywhere."

"I should have come by sooner," Padraig said at last. "I thought maybe you'd want some time to yourself. I won't make that mistake again."

She was taken aback by the guilt, the self-recrimination in his tone.

"You're not responsible for me," she said, trying to soften her words. She failed. Everything she said sounded like an accusation, which was ridiculous. What she said was true. Padraig, despite his vow of friendship, was basically a stranger.

Story of her life. She'd wasted her entire twenty-six years of existence, hanging out with strangers, never managing to form any close or lasting attachments. That was the one thing that kept coming back to her all weekend.

She was completely and utterly alone. And she had no one to blame for that but herself.

"Give me your hand," Padraig said, holding his out. His voice was quiet, gentle, and she responded to it before she could consider her actions.

The moment her fingers touched his, a sense of peace washed through her. He'd held her hand Friday night, and now, like then, the simple gesture relaxed her, gave her comfort.

"Can I be brutally honest with you?"

She nodded, her anger fading fast.

"If your doctor's diagnosis is right, we don't have the time we need to let this friendship grow naturally. That means we're going to have to start somewhere in the middle. Going to have to pretend we've known each other for years, rather than months. I went all through school with this girl, Kelli. We've been best friends since second grade. If I'm acting like a jackass, she has no trouble calling me out for it. And if I think she's doing something dangerous, I give her the what for. You can do that with people you've been friends with forever because the relationship is solid. Kelli has seen me pissed off, brokenhearted and drunk as a skunk. I've seen her in full-out bitch mode, I endured her brief skanky phase in tenth grade, and I've returned that drunk-as-a-skunk favor and held her hair while she threw up after she's gotten wasted."

Mia grinned. "I'd like to meet Kelli. She sounds pretty cool."

"I'll introduce you." Then he continued to explain what was on his mind. "My point is, you and I don't have a shared history. And we might not have the luxury of time..."

Mia scoffed, even though she liked how he kept saying "might." She'd seen the X-rays and she knew it wasn't a "might" or an "if," but there was something very comforting about the fact that he hadn't written her off yet.

She wished she could muster that same determination. Dig deep and find some sort of positive in this. Or at the very least, the energy to make her final days count for something.

Unfortunately, she wasn't there.

For the past few days, she'd tossed and turned on her couch, cursed God and Buddha, her mother, her sperm donor, and pretty much every other asshole who had ever looked through her rather than at her. At her lowest point, she'd taunted God to just go ahead and fucking kill her. Why bother with six months? What was he waiting for?

The worst part was…she still felt that way. Going through the motions, dealing with the worsening headaches, waiting and wondering if today was going to be the day she died, seemed like too much damn work for absolutely no reward.

What the hell did she have to live for?

It took her a few minutes to realize Padraig had stopped talking. She looked into his eyes and read the concern there.

"What?" she asked.

"You've already given up. You want to die now."

She flushed, wondering if Padraig could somehow read minds. Then she recalled his ability to read faces, to look at a person and know if they were sad or angry or…praying for death. For four months, she'd watched him ask all the right questions at the bar whenever a patron came in and ordered a drink.

She gave him the truth because she had nothing else left to lose at this point. "It would be a lot easier."

"I'm not letting you take the easy way out."

It occurred to her now how the room must really look to him—the drawn shades, the empty wine bottles, the spilled pills. "I didn't…I mean, I'm not planning to kill myself. I just think it would be easier if this tumor did whatever the fuck it's going to do, and…"

Padraig squeezed her hand, then used his hold to tug her closer. He was a tall guy, with broad shoulders and a muscular build that sent the message he could definitely take care of himself in a fight. When their faces were just a few inches away, she saw the fierce determination in his gaze.

"From now on, I'm going to talk to you like I would Kelli. We've been friends forever."

She wished that were true. Maybe her life would have turned out differently if she'd ever let someone get as close as Padraig had let Kelli.

"So as your forever friend, I'm putting my foot down. The pity party ends now. You're going to get a shower while I clean up this mess. You're going to put on some makeup, fix your hair, and then I'm taking you over to the pub for a hot meal. Maybe three hot meals. From the looks of you, I'd say you haven't eaten anything in days. And then you and I are going to make some plans for the future."

"That shouldn't take too long." Every time she thought the bitterness was under control, it found a way to seep out again.

"You get one of those a day. And that's it."

Mia grinned, completely enthralled by his heavy-handedness. No one had ever cared about her enough to tell her off, to put her in her place. The second anyone got too close, she backed away, made sure she was gone before they got too deep.

By skipping the trust-building phase, Padraig was thrusting her beyond her fears. Putting her in a place where the trust was assumed. Strangely, it wasn't freaking her out.

"What's the special tonight?" she asked, her stomach confirming what he'd just said. Now that he'd promised her food, she was starving.

"Lamb stew."

Her stomach rumbled again, the return of her appetite sudden and painful.

"I'll hurry." She started toward the hall, but stopped at the sound of him picking up the wine bottles. "You don't have to clean up. I can do that later."

"It'll give me something to do while I wait."

She attempted to stare him down, but Padraig turned away and continued tidying. He clearly wasn't the type of man to obey any order he didn't agree with.

Mia locked herself in the bathroom, peeling off the clothes she'd worn for too long, dumping the entire outfit in the trash, and then climbing under the hot water.

The heat and steam and soothing jets worked out the tiny bit of tension remaining. Padraig had taken care of the rest of her anxieties with his take-charge attitude.

She gave her hair and makeup a lick and a promise because hunger was winning the war against vanity. Padraig had done wonders with her living room, the place put back together perfectly by the time she returned. He'd opened the shades, allowing the last rays of sunlight in as afternoon gave way to evening. He'd taken the environment from dreary cave to cozy home once more.

"Ready?"

She nodded, pulled on her coat and accepted his outstretched hand. Holding his hand was starting to feel normal in addition to nice.

They talked about a whole lot of nothing on their way to the pub. She told him a little bit more about her work and he filled her in on the latest hockey scores. It did indeed look like his Caps were heading to the Stanley Cup playoffs. Of course, so were her Blackhawks. They were still trash-talking when they entered the pub.

Monday night was typically one of her usual nights at Pat's. Mainly because, like most everyone in the world, she hated the beginning of the work week, and she was tired at the end of the day. Plus, Mondays were slower at Pat's, so the fact she was eating alone week after week was obvious to fewer people.

She started to walk to her usual stool, but Padraig tugged on her hand, guiding her to a table right in the middle of the room. Mia smiled as she sat in the chair he pulled out for her. "Sorry. Habit."

He grinned at her. "Thought the table might be more private. My dad is manning the bar tonight and he's a terrible eavesdropper. Plus, Pop Pop is here to watch the game and he's nosier than an old woman. I suspect he'll be over soon under the guise of 'just saying hello'."

"Should I prepare myself for the Spanish Inquisition?"

Padraig shook his head. "No. I don't think it'll be anything as serious as that. He already knows the worst about you."

Mia's smile faded. "Oh."

Padraig sighed. "I wasn't talking about the tumor. I mean, he does know about that, but I was actually referring to your misplaced devotion to the Blackhawks."

Mia laughed, startling herself with the loudness and the actual joy behind it.

"My family sort of operates on a hive mind and a hive heart. I talked to my mom about your health concerns and it snowballed from there. Which means…they all know and they're all worried about you."

She tilted her head, confused. "They don't even know me."

Padraig seemed as flummoxed by her response as she was his. "You can't feel empathy or concern for strangers? Hell, I wouldn't even call you a stranger. When I mentioned your name, my dad and Pop Pop both knew exactly who you were, that you were from Chicago. That you were pretty and sweet."

She blushed at his compliment. "Is charm a Collins' trait as well?"

"It certainly is, young lady."

Mia and Padraig looked up, both trying not to laugh as his Pop Pop stood next to the table.

"That didn't take long," Padraig muttered.

"Patrick Collins," the older gentleman said, reaching out to shake her hand. "But you can call me Pat or Pop Pop."

"Pop Pop?" she asked. "I don't think—"

"Actually, I think I prefer that. So scratch the Pat part. You will call me Pop Pop."

Mia wasn't sure how to respond to yet another heavy-handed male. She would have thought that character trait a defect in a man, but somehow the Collins men made it feel appealing, and in Padraig's case—God help her—sexy.

Maybe her problem dealing with men in this situation was her upbringing. Her adult role models growing up had all been female. Hell, even her boss was a woman. She lacked experience in the Y chromosome world.

"It's very nice to meet you," she said.

"Padraig tells us you're from Chicago."

She nodded. "Yes. Born and raised."

"And you've moved to Baltimore because of a job opportunity?"

"I'm opening a satellite office for the company I've been working for the past five years. It's an office supply store. My boss is an amazing woman, very driven and savvy. She started out with one office, but now she has two branches in Chicago, one in Atlanta, and this one in Baltimore."

"She must think very highly of you and your work."

Mia blushed and shrugged. "I guess."

"No guessing about it. I like a person who isn't afraid to roll up their sleeves and work hard."

Mia smiled. The Collins men weren't shy when it came to giving compliments. Before she could reply, Padraig's dad appeared.

"You interrupting Padraig's date, Pop?"

Mia started to correct the man about this being a date, but Padraig spoke first.

"Dad, this is Mia. Mia, this is my dad, Tristan."

"Hello, Mr. Collins," she said."

"Tris," Padraig's dad corrected her. "Can I get the two of you something to drink?"

"I'll have a Guinness. Thanks. Mia?"

She typically drank white wine, but she liked the idea of trying something different tonight. "I think I'll have the same."

Tris appeared impressed as he turned to get their drinks.

"A Guinness girl, eh?" Mr. Collins was smiling at her, and she felt her fondness for the older man growing with each passing minute.

"I've actually never had it."

"You'll love it. Who knows? Taste of Irish goodness might clear your head and help you to see the light about those damn Blackhawks. Tsk tsk tsk. And, with that, I'll leave you two to your date."

Mia shook her head. "Oh, no. It's not like that. We're just…" She didn't bother to finish her sentence because Mr. Collins was already gone, settling back onto his stool at the bar, his gaze glued to the beginning of the hockey game.

Tris returned with their drinks, but like Pop Pop, he was clearly distracted by the game. He set the beers down with a quick "enjoy" and was back at the bar within seconds.

"Your family is very nice."

"Thanks."

She sort of expected Padraig to follow suit with his dad and Pop Pop and start watching the game. After all, he was a die-hard fan as well, and it was his beloved Caps playing. She was pleasantly surprised to discover all his attention was on her.

"We could move over to the bar if you wanted to watch the game with them. I don't mind."

He shook his head. "I've seen a million hockey games in my life, Mia. This one can go on without me. I actually brought you here so that we could—"

"Hey, Paddy."

They looked up to discover yet another relative next to the table.

Padraig sighed. "Mia, this is my aunt Riley. And," he paused for three seconds as a beautiful dark-haired woman approached as well, "my aunt Keira."

He looked over their shoulders as if searching for someone. "Where's Mom?"

Riley grinned. "Sitting over on Sunday's Side. We thought it might be annoying if we all just swooped around you at the same time."

Padraig rolled his eyes as Mia laughed.

"Hey, Mom," he called out loudly.

A head peeped around the corner, and Mia stood slowly as Padraig's mother walked over to their table.

"Mia, this is Lane," Riley said, taking over the introductions.

Mia hoped there wasn't a test later. She stretched out her hand, but Lane bypassed it, drawing her into a warm embrace.

"Padraig has filled me in on just a bit of what the doctor told you. I know your next appointment is tomorrow afternoon. I was thinking the two of us could go out to lunch beforehand and make a list of the questions you have."

Mia blinked rapidly, surprised by the sudden wash of tears. She was touched by the kindness being shown to her tonight. "That would be nice, but I don't mean to monopolize so much of your day."

Lane waved away her concern. "We're going to get the answers we need, Mia. After the consultation, we'll come back here and figure out our next course of action. Okay?"

The more Padraig's family offered to help her, the more Mia realized she never would have been able to do all of this on her own. "I'm not sure how to thank you—"

"No thanks necessary. Now, I'm going to take my sisters-in-law back to Sunday's Side and let you two get back to your date."

"It's not—" Mia started again, but Padraig drowned her words out once more.

"We'll both have the special, Aunt Riley." He looked at Mia. "You want an appetizer? Bread?"

She shook her head. After so long without food, she was worried about overeating. "Just the stew will be great."

Riley promised to bring the food right out and, once more, she and Padraig were alone. Not that Mia expected that to last long. Family members appeared to crawl out of the woodwork around here.

"I really do appreciate your mom's willingness to go see the doctor with me."

Padraig reached across the table and took her hand. "I'd like to go too, if that's alright with you."

"You don't have to do that."

"I know I don't have to. I want to. I have a bunch of questions for your doctor myself."

"Really?"

He nodded. "Yeah. Spent the better part of the weekend talking to my mom and looking some stuff up online. Apparently, treatment plans and such depend on the size and location of the tumor. And just because this guy doesn't see much hope—"

"Any," she corrected. "He doesn't see any."

Padraig frowned. "My mom has the name of a brain surgeon. One of the best in the country. She has some connections and thinks she can get you in to see him. We're not packing it in just yet."

Again with the word "we." Mia couldn't believe how such a tiny two-letter word could provoke such a powerful, overwhelming feeling of happiness inside her.

Padraig glanced around the room and, for a moment, she thought he actually looked a little nervous.

"Listen," he began. "Before any more of my family makes their way over here, I wanted to talk to you about something important."

"Okay."

"I've been giving a lot of thought to your list."

"My list?"

"The things you thought you would do before you died."

Mia recalled Friday night and how she'd rattled off all of her regrets. "Oh. Yeah. What about it?"

"I think I can help you achieve them."

She frowned. "Which ones?"

"All of them."

Mia considered his comment, then decided he must be joking. There was no way she could accomplish even half of the things she'd mentioned. "That's not possible."

"You're wrong."

She was starting to recognize Padraig's "stubborn" tone, the sound that emerged whenever he was determined to do whatever he wanted despite her arguments.

"Padraig," she argued, "I'm not even going to get past number one."

"Maybe not right away, but…"

"But?" she prodded.

"Let's focus on the others first. You have a passport?"

Mia nodded numbly, trying to figure out if Padraig was kidding or not. He'd promised her a lifelong friend, which for them meant two people with a pretend past and a short-term future.

"Good. We're going to tackle Paris by way of Harry Potter World."

"Florida isn't on the way to France."

Padraig laughed. "It will be the way we do it."

Mia fell silent when Riley appeared and placed a basket of freshly baked bread on their table. All she said was, "You look hungry," before she returned to the kitchen.

"Listen," Mia began. "I appreciate what you're trying to do. I'm actually overwhelmed by all of," she lifted her hands and gestured toward his family, "this. But you have your own life to live, Padraig. I don't expect you to put everything on hold just because I have this stupid tumor in my head." She rubbed her brow, realizing the dull ache that was always there was less painful tonight than it had been in a long time. Probably because Padraig was distracting her. Typically, she was alone with too much time to think. And feel.

"Hear me out, Mia. The other night, when you started making that list, I realized something."

"What's that?"

"None of us get any guarantees in life. I sat in your living room and listened to all your dreams, and I realized many of them were the same as mine. We have a chance to chase a few of them together."

"Padraig. I can assure you. I'm not going to be great company. In addition to my constant headaches, I'm bound to be an emotional train wreck. You can't honestly think that sounds like a good time."

He didn't appear to agree. "You can be anything you want to be, Mia. Happy, sad, angry. I suspect you'll be all of those in the months to come. But you have to remember something. Life isn't measured in years. It's measured in moments. I want to be there for your moments."

Mia swallowed heavily, certain she'd never heard a more beautiful request. If only they'd started talking before...

Before.

"You don't seriously expect me to believe Harry Potter World was on your bucket list," she said, trying to lighten the moment, trying to make this very sweet man understand that, while she would be forever grateful for his kindness, she couldn't let him turn his world upside down for her.

Padraig gave her a wicked grin. "I can go upstairs right now and bring down my Seamus Finnigan wand."

She laughed. "Please tell me you're kidding. Who owns a Seamus wand?"

"Might have been a gag gift from my brother Colm for Christmas a couple of years ago. Got drunk one night during a Harry Potter marathon—okay, drinking game, my cousins have issues when it comes to parties—and went on a rant about how Voldemort never would have made it to book seven if there'd been more Irish in the series."

Mia pressed her hand over her mouth, trying not to keep laughing. "I'm not going to lie. That explanation just raises more questions in my mind. You were playing a Harry Potter drinking game?"

"We took a shot of whiskey every time they said He Who Must Not Be Named."

"First of all, that's sacrilegious, and I hope you'll invite me the next time you play. Colm seriously got you a Seamus wand?"

He nodded.

"I didn't even know they made a Seamus one."

"Had my Irish on that night. The name Seamus always reminds me of an old Irish folktale my Pop Pop told me when I was a kid. Not going to lie. Colm gave the wand to me as a joke, but I like it. Feel like maybe there's a bit of magic fighting to get out of me."

"Okay, you've convinced me," she said, giving in. "Maybe Harry Potter *is* on your list, but Paris?"

"You're joking, right? Tour de France? FIFA?"

Mia shook her head. "It's beginning to occur to me that I'll never win an argument with you."

Padraig leaned back in his chair, lacing his fingers behind his head. "Good. Glad we've crossed that bridge early. Now we can stop wasting time."

"What bridge?"

"The one where you keep fighting me. Here's what's going to happen next. We're going to the doctor tomorrow and getting some answers. If this is something we can fight, we will."

"And if not?" she forced herself to ask.

"We start working our way down that bucket list.

Chapter Five

April 3

Padraig wiped up the counter with a vengeance as he replayed everything that had happened yesterday. The visit to Dr. Richards hadn't gone the way he'd hoped.

Somewhere between Friday night and Tuesday afternoon, he'd convinced himself the doctor had been wrong. He'd imagined walking into that office and discovering that Mia had misunderstood some part of the diagnosis and cure. He'd been convinced there was something that could save her. After all, modern medicine was finding cures to diseases every day, discovering new ways to perform surgery, so how could there still be such a thing as an inoperable brain tumor?

She was too young, too healthy, too...well, she was too great to die.

So he'd convinced himself it had all been some big mistake. When Dr. Richards confirmed that Mia's hearing and understanding were just fine, he'd latched on to the next piece of hope—the second opinion.

Dr. Richards agreed to send Mia's records to the specialist his mom knew, but last night, after they'd dropped Mia off at her apartment, his mom had come back to the pub with him, joined him at the bar for a

Guinness, and warned him not to get his hopes up in that very gentle voice she used when she knew he was destined for disappointment.

Since then, he'd been walking around in a state of rage, barking at anyone who got in his way.

"You're not answering your phone. You keep sending me to voicemail."

He looked up at Kelli and scowled. She'd called a few times since Saturday, but he'd ignored her. Part of him was afraid she'd call him a fool for his determination to marry Mia.

No, he wasn't afraid of her telling him that. He was more afraid of realizing she was right.

He'd lived his entire life under a lucky star, more often than not, finding a way to get anything he wanted. It didn't look like that was going to happen this time—and he was pissed as fuck.

"Wow." Kelli sat down at the bar. "Who peed in your cornflakes?"

"I didn't answer the phone because I'm not in the mood to chitchat."

"Yeah," Kelli said, not taking heed of the dark tone in his voice. "I can see that. So...what's wrong?"

"Nothing," he grumbled, turning away from her.

"Try again."

"Goddammit, Kell. Why can't you catch a fucking clue?"

"Is it that Brooke woman? Did she dump you? Want me to go kick her ass?"

Kelli had been his friend too many years to be afraid of his foul moods. He'd foolishly told Mia this was the kind of relationship he wanted with *her*. Now he was reconsidering. There was something to be said about the ability to scare people away. "It's not Brooke."

"Yeah. I didn't think you were that into her. So what is it? You and Colm in a fight?"

He shook his head. Her guessing was wearing him out. It was also diffusing his fury. "No. We're fine."

"Well, I know it's not the Caps because they won last night. And I know it's not me, because I'm fucking awesome, so I give up. Why are you being a dick?"

His shoulders slumped, resignation creeping in. He sort of preferred the rage. "I just got some bad news about a friend."

Kelli frowned. "Oh man. I'm sorry. What happened?"

"One of our regulars." He paused. Calling Mia a regular felt wrong. Like he was downplaying who she was. "A friend of mine has been diagnosed with an inoperable brain tumor. She's dying."

"Shit," Kelli whispered. "Who?"

"Her name is Mia Curtis. She usually sits—"

Kelli cut him off, pointing toward Mia's usual spot. "Oh my God! The redhead from Chicago?"

He nodded, stunned. "How the hell do *you* know who she is?" Kelli was also a regular at the pub, but she typically sat at a table with his cousins or her friends from work.

Kelli Peterson was Mia's complete opposite when it came to social circles. Mia's were small—practically nonexistent—while Kelli seemed to know and like every single person in the city.

"She was always here on competition nights when *February Stars* was going on. I was standing next to her one night, waiting for your slow ass to fix me a drink, and we started talking." Kelli gave him a wicked grin and wiggled her eyebrows. "We hung out once or twice during the shows after that. Damn. I really like her."

He rolled his eyes and imagined their conversations. "Let me guess, you were both going on and on about how fine Hunter's ass is. You're going to have to rein in that lust whenever Ailis is around."

"Why?" Kelli asked. "Ailis and I have had countless discussions about Hunter's ass, and she agrees with me. Anyway, Mia and I only chatted a couple times—I don't even think I told her my name, and only knew *hers* because you said it when you brought her a drink. And we didn't chat about Hunter. It was about you."

"Me?"

"The first time, you were in the midst of some big debate with Finn, regarding the odds on all the bets being placed on the competition. I think she thought the two of you were fighting, and she was worried. I explained that trash talk and gambling were part of the Collins family fabric, and you were essentially a dopey, oversized puppy dog who wouldn't hurt a flea."

Padraig blew out an annoyed breath. "Thanks a lot. You go on and on about Hunter's fine ass and all I get is dopey, oversized puppy dog. You suck as a wingman. Which is why Colm will remain best man in my wedding."

Kelli had been begging Padraig to drop his twin like a bad habit when he finally decided to get married, volunteering to stand in as best woman. They'd teased each other about it for years, Padraig holding it over her head every time she annoyed him.

"How was I supposed to know you were interested? Last I heard, the new girl's name was Brooke. I didn't realize you and Mia even knew each other that well."

They didn't. And yet, somehow Padraig was starting to feel like he knew Mia better than anyone.

Mia had remained calm throughout the visit with the doctor, finding a strength he knew he'd never possess. She asked good questions, listened intently to the answers and, throughout all of it, never fell apart. Not even when they were back in the car.

Instead, she and his mom chatted about Dr. Richards' responses and the specialist. When they got back to her place, she thanked them for going with her and told them she was going to have to take some time to consider her options.

Options. The moment she'd said the word, Padraig's anger sparked.

What fucking options?

Die in six months without treatment or die in eight to ten months with needles in your arm and poison creeping through your veins.

"Jesus. There's that murderous gleam in your eyes again. You should hit the gym. Or more specifically, the heavy bag. You keep this kind of aggression pent up much longer and you'll explode."

He nodded slowly. Padraig belonged to a boxing club, but getting into a ring with a living, breathing human being would only ensure he hurt someone. The heavy bag was a good call.

"Yeah. I'll do that later."

"So, Mia..." Kelli prompted, still waiting to hear why he was so upset about someone he hadn't even really known a week earlier.

"We've been talking a lot since Friday," he explained. "She has a bucket list."

Kelli's expression softened. "How long does she have?"

"Six months or so."

"Shit," Kelli whispered again. Padraig wasn't surprised by the tears he saw gathering in her eyes. Kelli, for all her tough exterior, was pure marshmallow inside.

"Yeah. I'm going to help her chisel away at everything on that list, make sure she doesn't die with any regrets."

"I think that's awesome, Paddy. To tell you the truth, if it was me, and I only had months to live, there's no one else I'd rather spend that time with."

He gave her a disbelieving look. Their friendship—while tight—was based more on playful insults and putdowns. Compliments were few and far between. Primarily because they both got embarrassed whenever the other said anything nice. Sarcasm was their first language, English a distant second.

Before last week, he would have teased her for the kindness, found a way to twist it back to humor. Today, the words sank bone-deep, gave him a glimpse of hope again.

Maybe the hope wasn't going to be found in a cure. Maybe it was going to come from something else.

"Thanks, Kell. I needed to hear that."

She flushed and shrugged. "My primary purpose in life is to keep you grounded and humble. And believe me, I find that easier than building you up in weak moments, so you're gonna have to get your shit together, okay? Mia needs a friend who isn't walking around like a bear with a thorn in his paw."

"Yeah. I guess she does." But it was starting to occur to him that maybe he needed Mia too. She'd opened his eyes to some hard truths about the way he was living his own life. With youth came an erroneous but unwavering belief in immortality. Nothing was certain, yet he'd meandered through his own adult life like he had all the time in the world.

And he'd spent the last decade hanging out behind this bar, waiting for life to come to *him*.

What an idiot.

He took a deep breath. "One of the things on her list is to get married."

"Whoa. Wait a minute. You're going to propose?"

"Yeah. I think I am. Not right away. God, she'd think I was crazy and turn me down if I asked now. We hardly know each other. But her list…"

"Got you thinking, huh?"

"You and I are both thirty-one, Kell. I keep waiting for this 'a-ha' moment where I'm instantly grown up. Then another year passes and I'm still living above the family pub. I look at Mia and I see the chance to do something real. Something that matters. Not just to her, but to me."

Kelli fell silent, something that didn't happen often. Usually her mouth was moving before her brain, so the fact that she was thinking about her next comment was all the warning he needed.

This was why he'd avoided her calls. She was too damn good at giving voice to the warning bells in his own head that he often ignored.

"She's dying, Paddy."

He winced. Hearing those words kept getting harder.

"I understand that you want to get married. Hell, I do too. But there's really only one reason to get married that's acceptable in my mind. And that's love. Take the next few months and work your way through this bucket list. Get to know her and let her get to know you. All of that is fine. But if you're serious about your intentions, in addition to that, you have to do something else, something that's harder."

"What?"

"You have to open up your heart to her, Paddy. Don't be afraid to let yourself fall in love with her if that's where it's heading. You've spent most of your adult life looking for the perfect relationship, something like what your mom and dad have. And I've gotta give you props. You're always giving it the college try. But proposing to this woman because it's on her bucket list and she's dying is fucking cheating. She doesn't deserve that. Of course, I think you already know that. It's why you've been avoiding my calls."

"You always go for the jugular." There was no heat behind his words...because she was right. And he appreciated the fact she cared enough to always tell him the truths he didn't want to hear.

"Yeah, well, you've left me bleeding a few times too. And as much as it pains me to admit it, you were always right to give me the jab."

"She doesn't call it her bucket list. She thinks of it as a list of regrets, of things she'll never accomplish."

"And that's eating your inner Boy Scout alive. You're a giver, Paddy. You always have been. But life is a pretty solid yin and yang. Light and darkness. Love and hate. Satisfaction and regret. You can't cure her, but you can be her friend. You can help her through the next few months, even if that means you only help her achieve *some* of the things on her list."

"What if I do fall in love with her?"

He hadn't meant to ask that question, to give that idea a voice. But the more time he spent with Mia, the more he started to believe he was in definite danger of falling for her.

"Then you'll tie the knot. And I'll be there with bells on."

He grinned, finding the opening he needed to return them to normal. "Damn, Kell. Bells could be a bit loud."

"Tell you what. If you, my dearest and oldest— though somewhat dim-witted—best friend since second grade, fall for this woman, I'll perform the ceremony."

Padraig chuckled, the sound feeling downright rusty. "Kelli—"

"You pretty much have to let me. Since you insist on giving Colm the gig of best man, it's either he and I engage in a fight to the death, or you let me be the officiant. I kind of like the idea of coming up with your vows for you. Speaks to the power-hungry bitch inside me."

"It's a deal."

"Excellent. Okay, I'm off. Gotta work the book fair at the library tonight."

Try as he may, Padraig always struggled to picture his best friend as a kindergarten teacher. It wasn't that she wasn't great with kids. She was. But more often than not, the Kelli he saw was showing off her tattoos in tight tank tops, cussing like a sailor and kicking his ass at flip cup.

"And for future reference, if you're hoping to avoid me, the surest way to fail at that is to ignore my phone calls."

He saluted. "So noted."

Kelli started toward the door, but it took her a full ten minutes to leave the pub because she stopped at no less than three tables to talk.

There was obviously a reason why she was his best friend. She could always cheer him up.

He filled a few more drink orders, then called in one of the part-time bartenders. Pretty soon, if he kept skipping out on shifts, he was going to owe everyone in the pub favors.

Once his replacement arrived, he headed over to Sunday's Side. His parents were enjoying a quiet dinner together. He grabbed the seat across the booth from them.

"Where are you headed off to?" his dad asked. "Who's manning the bar?"

"Called Joel in to work. I'm going to pop over to Mia's to check on her. I wanted to talk to you about the schedule, Dad."

"Okay."

"I'd like to take some time off."

His mother smiled, reaching across the table to squeeze his hand. "I think that's a good idea, Paddy. You started working at the pub in high school, and while Colm has taken some vacations, traveled and seen a bit of the world, you never really have. It's a good time to widen your borders, see how others live."

He nodded, glad his mom was so supportive. "Mia wants to see Paris. And Harry Potter World."

Tris laughed. "I can see Mia wanting to visit Paris, but are you sure Harry Potter was *her* idea?"

Padraig grinned. "I'm not going to pretend that part of the trip will be a hardship. You know how much I love theme parks and roller coasters. Add in a trip to Hogwarts and I'll be in hog heaven."

"Take the time, son. It'll be good for Mia and you."

Padraig stood, thanking his dad. Before he made it two steps from the table, his dad said, "I'm proud of you, Paddy."

Padraig nodded, choking down yet another emotion. He was on a roll today. First anger, then amusement and now this. "Enjoy your dinner."

He threw on his coat and headed for Mia's apartment. She wasn't expecting him, but even so, he didn't text or call to warn her that he was on his way.

He was afraid to. Afraid she'd succumbed to the same depression that had swallowed her the past weekend and she'd tell him not to come. He was finding it harder and harder to stay away, to leave her alone for any amount of time at all.

When he stood outside her door, he paused, surprised by the sound of music. Listening closely, he was certain he could hear her singing along. He smiled as he listened to her belting out Adele. For the life of him, he couldn't figure out what it was about that woman's songs that made most women he knew stop everything and fly into Whitney Houston mode, singing like their lives depended on it.

He knocked.

Mia obviously hadn't given in to depression again. She was in sweatpants, a T-shirt, and her hair was pulled back in a ponytail. "Hey, Padraig. What are you doing here? I thought you had work."

He glanced over her shoulder. She was clearly spring-cleaning. The vacuum was out and every piece of furniture was gleaming.

"Expecting company?" That was pretty much the only reason he and his cousins ever went into this kind of deep-cleaning mode.

"No. My grandma used to call this nesting. Woke up this morning and thought I'd better take some time to get my shit together." She walked over to the coffee table and picked up a notepad. "I've been making a list of things I need to take care of. I don't have a will, which isn't really a big deal considering I don't own anything. But I need to figure out funeral arrangements and stuff like that."

Her tone as she spoke about planning her own funeral was too matter-of-fact. He'd heard people talk about the weather with more emotion. It didn't help that hearing her mention wills and funerals made him want to throw up.

Padraig took the notepad away from her and flipped the page. "I'm glad you're in the mood to make plans, because that's why I'm here."

She narrowed her eyes. He hadn't brought up his intention to tackle her bucket list since Monday night, but it was clear she hadn't forgotten. Or changed her mind. "Padraig, I don't think—"

"You have a laptop?"

She nodded.

"Good. Grab it. Time to do some research. Book a couple flights."

"Padraig. What about Brooke? How is she going to feel about you running off with some other woman to a foreign country?"

He lifted one shoulder casually. "I called her Saturday. Told her I couldn't see her anymore."

She gasped. "Call her back! You like her. There's no way I'd screw that up for you."

"No. I'm not calling her back. She was fine, Mia. The two of us weren't serious. She hadn't met my family, and to be perfectly honest, I hadn't even gotten past second base."

"Which base is second again?"

He laughed but ignored her question, getting straight to the heart of things. "I haven't taken a real vacation since high school graduation, and before that, it was just trips to the river, beach, or amusement parks with my folks and brother. So really, when you think about it, I'm doing this as much for me as you."

"Do *you* have a passport?"

He nodded. "Got one a year or so ago. Colm and I have this pipe dream that one day we'll take Pop Pop back to Ireland."

"That would be wonderful."

"Yeah. We'd really like to see where he grew up. Not sure it'll ever happen, but I wanted to have my passport just in case."

She didn't move to grab the laptop, and he realized he'd made an assumption about something she hadn't mentioned yet.

"If you want to stay here and start the chemo, Mia, I'll be with you every step of the way."

She shook her head. "No. I'm not doing that."

She had said as much yesterday. He understood her reasoning, but her hesitance made him wonder if she'd reconsidered. Dr. Richards had suggested a very powerful dose of chemotherapy, one that would certainly make her sick. One that would cause her hair to fall out. And in the end, Dr. Richards said it would only buy her months, not years.

Mia insisted quality won out over quantity.

"Will you be able to take some time off to travel? I know you're in a new position."

Mia's eyes got misty as she nodded. "I called Phyllis last night and explained what was happening. I wasn't sure what to do about work. She told me to take some time off to get my affairs in order. She wouldn't let me quit because she said she's not about to leave me without health insurance."

"I like Phyllis."

Mia smiled. "Me too."

"If you're hesitating because of money—" He had some, and Aunt Teagan called him from New York on Tuesday morning to assure him that she and Sky would pay for Paris if he and Mia didn't have enough. At the time, he'd been amused by how quickly word had spread in his family, still riding the "she's not really dying" high. Now he was determined to make sure nothing stood in their way.

"I'm not," she said. "I inherited some money from my grandma, and one of the benefits of having very little social life includes the ability to stash away money from my paycheck each month."

"We're taking the trip, Mia."

He expected her to continue to resist, but when she sat down and pulled her laptop out of its case, he hooted.

Her funeral list was forgotten as they spent the next four hours planning her dream trips to Florida and France.

Chapter Six

April 17

Padraig pulled up a stool next to his Pop Pop at the bar. It was a rare occasion when he could sit on this side of the counter with his grandfather. He lifted his pint glass and tapped it against the older man's.

"Great party," Padraig said, aware that he'd be wise to follow this pint with a glass of water if he stood a chance at feeling okay tomorrow. He didn't relish the idea of flying to Florida hungover.

"It is indeed," Pop Pop said, looking over his shoulder toward Mia on the dance floor.

Padraig followed his line of vision and grinned. Mia was probably past the point of feeling well in the morning—water or not. But it was obvious she felt fine now, and Padraig figured that was more important.

The past two weeks had been a roller coaster of emotions. The visit to the specialist had yielded the expected outcome, his prognosis matching that of Dr. Richards'.

Mia had actually taken that news better than Padraig. She sat through the visit stoically and remained quiet on the drive home. She had asked for some time alone and Padraig had granted it.

Then he'd headed straight to the Collins Dorm and punched a hole in the living room wall.

Since then, they'd both distracted themselves with work and vacation plans, not mentioning her illness at all.

Padraig had promised to treat her as he did Kelli, to act as if they'd been friends forever, but the more time he spent with Mia, the more he found that pretense unnecessary. Their friendship came easily, naturally. He was able to say things to her he'd never told anyone else, and she'd confided she felt the same.

He had actually spent the last few nights kicking himself for not starting some more meaningful conversations with her earlier. She'd been sitting at the end of his bar for months, and he'd failed to see how cool she was.

Pop Pop continued to watch the girls on the dance floor. "Mia looks like she's having a good time."

Padraig chuckled. "I'm worried my cousins are being a bad influence on her."

"No. I get the feeling Mia hasn't had much experience with cutting loose and having a good time. The girls are just showing her the way."

His grandfather made a good point. Yvonne and Sunnie had grabbed Mia's hands the second she'd arrived for their bon voyage party, taking control of her fun for the evening. The three of them, plus Kelli, had kept up a pretty intense routine of tequila shots followed by frenetic dancing.

The party had been Riley's idea, and unsurprisingly the rest of the family had been on board. They'd closed the pub down for the night, decorated the area behind the bar with a huge Bon Voyage sign, made a pile of food and a cake shaped like the Eiffel Tower, and even managed to get Sky and Teagan back in town for the evening to perform.

Padraig had kept their attendance at the party a secret, wanting to surprise Mia, whose eyes had nearly popped out of her head when she saw them onstage. She'd gone adorably shy when he had taken her over to introduce her to them.

Mia's cheeks were flushed from the exertion of dancing and she was grinning from ear to ear. She'd never looked prettier, more alive.

"She does look like she's having fun," Padraig said, his eyes widening as Mia started twerking. He laughed loudly. "Jesus. What's that?"

Pop Pop didn't bother to look. He gaze was locked on Padraig as he patted him on the shoulder. "I've always said when a Collins man falls, he falls fast and hard."

Padraig gave his grandfather a quizzical look, then realized Pop Pop was referring to him and Mia.

"Oh no," he said quickly. "It's not like that. We're just friends, Pop Pop."

"Mmmhmm," Pop Pop hummed, clearly not convinced. "What about the marriage proposal you were hell bent on issuing a couple weeks ago?"

Padraig sighed, suddenly regretting the way he'd just blurted that intention out to his whole family. In truth, he hadn't mentioned the idea of marrying Mia since his talk with Kelli. He'd always been too impetuous, and the morning after Mia's revelation, he'd been too keyed up on emotions and caffeine and lack of sleep to think it through clearly. Kelli had helped him see the error of his ways.

"I, uh…well…"

"You won't marry her if you're not in love with her."

He nodded slowly. "It was pointed out to me that my initial plan was based on a knee-jerk reaction to some pretty powerful emotions, coupled with my," he rolled his eyes, "Boy Scout nature."

Pop Pop laughed. "Who got to you first? Colm or Kelli?"

"Kelli," he admitted begrudgingly.

Pop Pop slapped him on the shoulder. "She's still gunning for best woman at your wedding, eh?"

"Yeah."

"She gave you good advice. Of course, I'm fairly certain the outcome will remain the same."

Padraig frowned. "What do you mean?"

"You're still going to marry that girl."

"But I just said I'm not going to marry her without love."

Pop Pop gave him that endearing, annoying smile that always told Padraig he was thick as a brick. "And I said, when a Collins falls, he falls fast and hard. You're no exception, son."

"I've only really known her three weeks."

"You think she's pretty though, don't you?"

Padraig looked across the bar, grinning at Mia's almost tangible joy. She and Yvonne were singing along to "Pretty Woman," using beer bottles as microphones. "She's beautiful."

"And sweet?"

"The sweetest girl I've met in a long time. She's funny too, but she doesn't realize it. Like I'll make a joke and she'll laugh and it'll catch her off guard, so she covers her mouth like—"

Padraig looked back just in time to catch Pop Pop's eye roll.

"Pop Pop. I'm not in love with her."

"I believe you. I also think you should end that proclamation with a 'yet.' You're not in love with her yet. But you're definitely seeing her. And something tells me she's never really experienced that. The beauty of being seen."

"I'm not sure I understand—"

"Love opens a person's eyes. Allows them to see things others might have missed. I think you've skirted around with love in the past, felt genuine affection for some of your old girlfriends."

"If that's true, why am I not married to one of them?"

"You weren't ready. Maybe your eyes were open, but your heart wasn't quite there. Or your heart was engaged, but hers wasn't. There are lots of reasons why love doesn't stick."

"And you think Mia's going to be the one to stick?" Padraig liked that idea more than he cared to admit.

"Only you can answer that, my boy. But I can tell you this—she sees you too. I've been watching her, and I guarantee you not a full five minutes has passed since she's arrived where she hasn't taken a moment to stop, look around, and find you."

Padraig didn't bother to hide the smile that little tidbit provoked. "Really?" he asked, looking behind him.

Sure enough, this time Mia was looking at him too. She gave him a goofy grin and a wave.

"Teagan's just caught sight of you," Pop Pop said after a minute or so. "I suspect..." He paused, then raised his hand to stop Padraig speaking. "Yep. There it is. A slow song. Go ask your gal to dance."

Padraig didn't bother with the pretense of resisting the suggestion. Pop Pop knew him too well, knew he wanted this dance.

He stood up and grasped Mia's hand, just as she was leaving the dance floor to return to her table for more tequila.

"Dance with me."

She smiled and stepped into his arms, and Padraig realized his grandfather was right.

Collins men fell hard and fast.

They swayed to the music, neither of them speaking. Instead, they just held tight.

Once the song ended, Teagan and Sky announced they were taking a break, which meant Riley spotted an unattended microphone. She stepped onstage and lifted her pint glass.

"Come on," Padraig said, leading Mia to the bar. "Riley's in a toasting mood. We need drinks in our hands."

Mia giggled as he handed her the beer his dad helpfully supplied.

Riley tapped the mic just once before speaking. "Someone once said that money spent on travel is never wasted, and I believe that's true. Our Paddy and dear Mia are off on a grand adventure. I've been blessed to go on more than a few wild rides with my sexy hubby, Aaron, over the years, so I'm speaking from experience when I say don't put limits on yourselves. Go to the casinos, the strip clubs, the seedy bars if you want."

Aaron groaned loudly. "Stay out of the seedy bars."

Everyone laughed, but Riley wasn't deterred. "I would remind the two of you that the journey is more important than the destination, but you've picked some pretty amazing places to visit, so I fear that won't be true. Take lots of pictures. Drop us a postcard. And I hope you find nothing but sunshine, delicious food, chilled wine, and don't forget to bring me back a souvenir." Then Riley turned to point a warning finger in Padraig's direction. "But not a wand. I don't want a stupid wand."

Padraig placed his hand over his heart as if she'd wounded him.

"Bon voyage!" Riley added as everyone repeated the words, clinked glasses and took a drink in their honor.

Padraig lifted his beer and tapped his glass against Mia's.

"You ready for this?" he asked.

She grinned eagerly. "So ready."

***

As the night grew later, Sky and Teagan slowed down the pace. Mia covered her mouth to hide her yawn, then took a long drink of water. She considered all the tequila she'd consumed, but couldn't summon an ounce of regret. It might actually be a nice change to have a headache caused by something other than a tumor. She could count on one hand the number of hangovers she'd had in her life, and all of those had come following a night of overindulging on wine...alone. Tonight had been all about family and friends and fun. The hangover would be so worth it.

"Want to take a spin with me on the floor?"

Mia looked up, her mind struggling to process the request. The face looking at her was Padraig's, but it wasn't his voice, and Colm didn't have the same mischievous twinkle in his eyes.

"Sure," she said, surprised by the invitation. While he seemed like a perfectly pleasant guy, she and Colm had never exchanged more than a few polite words over the past couple of weeks.

She took his hand as he led her to the dance floor.

"Sounds like you and Paddy are going to have a great trip."

She nodded. Honestly, she was so excited about their vacation she could hardly stand the wait. She was grateful they'd finally be on their way tomorrow afternoon.

"I hope you won't take this the wrong way, Mia, because the truth is I think you're a very nice person and the cards you've been dealt are just, well…fucking bullshit, if you'll forgive the expression."

The two of them continued to sway to the music, but his grip on her had loosened so that they could look at each other, face-to-face. Suddenly she understood the reason for the dance. It gave Colm a chance to speak to her in relative privacy. "You're worried about Padraig?"

"My brother is probably the nicest guy on the planet. He'd give you the shirt off his back. Hell, he'd give a person his shirt, pants, shoes and wallet, and walk home naked if someone needed his help."

"He's a protector," she said. Though her acquaintance with Padraig had been relatively short, that fact had been readily apparent very early on.

"More than that, he's a giver. And I don't just mean material stuff. I mean emotionally. The guy doesn't hold back. I've watched my brother take on everyone else's pain, working overtime to make someone laugh or to comfort them or to protect them. It's like he can't stop himself. That need is a part of him, like it's sewn into his skin or something."

She'd been on the receiving end of Padraig's compassion, his empathy. She knew all about his amazing ability to heal another person's soul. He'd dragged her out of dark places several times in just the past few weeks. There was no way she could deny that she already found herself relying on him, needing him. "You're afraid I'm using him."

Colm shook his head. "No. Not...not really. Not consciously."

"I *am* using him," she admitted. "He keeps offering me his shoulder, and I can't seem to stop myself from taking it."

"You're a good person, Mia. That's not really what this conversation is about. All I'm trying to say— badly—is that he's gonna give you everything he thinks you need because that's the kind of guy he is. He'll do it gladly, without a thought to what it's going to do to him in the long run."

"I'm going to die, Colm."

"And Padraig is going to be devastated."

"You think I should walk away from him? Now? Before we get any closer?"

Colm looked over his shoulder, searching for Padraig. Mia followed his direction, both of them spotting Padraig kicked back and laughing at something Finn had said. Then he saw them looking at him and gave them a goofy thumbs-up.

"You know what? Forget it. Forget every stupid thing I just said."

"Why?" she asked.

"Because I'm a fucking idiot."

He wasn't. Mia respected Colm for what he was doing. Everything he said was true. And as Padraig's brother, Colm felt his own need to protect. Even if he meant he was trying to protect Padraig from himself.

She started to tell him all of that, but Colm's next words stopped her.

"And because it's already too late."

The music ended, so Colm gave her another quick apology, thanked her for the dance and handed her over to Padraig, who was standing at the edge of the floor.

"Ready to call it a night?" Padraig asked. "It's getting late, and even though our flight isn't until late afternoon, I figure we should probably try to get some sleep tonight. I'm going to want to hit the ground running when we get there."

She nodded. "Yeah. Let me grab my coat."

"I'll say goodbye to my folks and meet you at the door."

A few minutes later, they were on their way. Padraig held her hand as they walked across the cobblestone street, enjoying the quiet night. Her head was still spinning from the alcohol, the dancing, and Colm's comments.

"I know Pat's Pub isn't exactly a nightclub, but I can't help but think you marked an item off your list tonight."

Mia considered his words and recalled her desire to dance with reckless abandon. "I did. Actually, I marked off two."

Padraig frowned, confused. "Two?"

"I also marked off the one where Sky and Teagan perform a private concert just for me."

He laughed. "Was that on the list?"

"If I'd realized it was possible, it would have been number one on the list."

Padraig stopped when they reached her building, his grin infectious. "I see how it is now. You're just going to keep adding things to the list. Okay. I'm in. I accept the challenge. What's next? Major motion picture premiere? Fancy a walk on the red carpet? The sky's the limit, Mia. Do your worst."

Colm's words drifted back to her. "I'm not your responsibility, Padraig," she said softly, aware that he really would continue to move heaven and earth to make her last few months happy.

"You're not my responsibility," he said slowly. "You're my friend. There's a big difference."

She watched the proverbial light come on as his smile turned to a scowl.

"What did my brother say to you?"

"Nothing I didn't need to hear. He loves you. That makes him protective."

"I'm going to kill him."

She laughed lightly as she put her hand on his arm to stop him from heading back to the pub to do just as he threatened. "No, you're not. He's looking out for you like you're looking out for me. Besides, he pointed out some things I hadn't considered before."

"Like what?" His tone was still deep with anger.

"When I first found out about the tumor, I didn't have anywhere to go, anyone to turn to. Then I walked into the pub and all of that changed. Maybe my perspective is skewed, because God knows time takes on an entirely different meaning when there's so little left. We've been moving in fast-forward for weeks."

He nodded slowly. "I just want to make sure we have time…" He paused as if searching for his words carefully. "Time to do everything you want to do."

She squeezed his hand as she smiled. "Tonight and this trip will be enough, Padraig. I'd rather slow things down, enjoy each moment rather than race to the next place in pursuit of ticking items off a list. This trip is enough," she repeated. And then, God help her, they would come home and she would do her damnedest to try to find a way to stop leaning on Padraig. To stand on her own two feet.

"Okay," he said at last, though it was obvious he didn't like what he was agreeing to.

"See you tomorrow. Around noon."

"Noon." Padraig reached out and pulled her into a big bear hug. She sucked in a deep breath of his yummy scent, beer and bourbon and the faded remnants of his cologne. Funny how she was becoming used to his smell, and how it made her feel safe and cherished.

He held her just a bit longer than usual, and it was Mia who had to break the embrace. It was hard pushing herself out of his arms.

It's already too late.

Colm's words drifted through her mind. She was beginning to fear he was right. And not in the way he meant.

It *was* already too late.

For her.

Padraig had snuck in under her radar and claimed a bit of her heart. Trying to keep any sort of emotional distance between them was going to be the hardest thing she'd ever have to do.

Even harder than dying at twenty-six.

Chapter Seven

April 20

Mia stood on a small bridge in the middle of the Universal theme park and looked at the Hogwarts castle. Padraig stood next to her. They'd walked by it countless times today as they'd rushed from ride to ride, laughing like a couple of teenagers skipping class for some grand adventure.

"I can't believe I'm standing here." She had said the exact same thing six hours earlier when they'd first walked into the park's replica of Harry Potter's Hogsmeade.

Padraig hadn't overplayed his love for all things Harry Potter. Something that made the incredibly kind man even more charming. It was sweet that he didn't even attempt to hide his affection for a children's series. "It's incredible, isn't it? Seeing all of it real and up close. It looks just like the movies."

The day was winding down. The park was going to close in a few minutes and sadly, Mia was starting to feel the effects of all her reveries. The dull ache in her head that started after lunch was now a pulsing throb that was getting harder to ignore.

"My grandma read the first Harry Potter book to me so many times we lost count. I loved it more than I can say. She'd no sooner say 'the end' before I was begging her to read it again. She always would. She loved the story too."

Padraig grasped her hand and gave it a squeeze. "I'll admit I was one of those who came to the books via the movies, as an adult. It was my cousin Darcy's fault. She's about ten years younger than me. I got roped into watching her one rainy afternoon when no one else could babysit. She wanted to watch the first movie, so we did. We were halfway through the second film when Aunt Riley got home. I stayed there until it was over. Then the next day I went out and bought the books."

"There's just something about them, isn't there?"

He nodded.

"After my grandmother died, they were the only things that made me still feel connected to her. Life was shit at home, and I sort of started imagining myself as Harry living with the Dursleys. I didn't have a real Hogwarts to escape to, so whenever stuff got bad or unbearable with my mom, I locked myself in my room and read for hours."

Padraig's expression sobered, as it often did whenever she spoke of her mother.

She squeezed his hand and smiled. "It's okay, Padraig. What's that saying? That which does not kill us makes us stronger. I'm not letting my mom ruin today. It's all been too perfect."

"Yeah. It has. But I might have a better quote."

"Oh yeah?" she asked, intrigued. It was rare to catch Padraig in a serious moment. He smiled and joked and laughed often, so his sudden seriousness captured her attention.

"Happiness can be found even in the darkest of times, if one only remembers to turn on the light."

Mia sucked in a deep breath as Dumbledore's advice took on a different meaning. "Padraig..."

"I started doing a reread of the books once the plans for this trip fell into place. I came across that line and I..." He swallowed. "It just sort of hit me as something important. Something that meant more than I realized the first time I read it."

She glanced over her shoulder at the castle and, for a moment, she could almost imagine her grandmother's voice issuing that advice. "Turn on the light, Tilly Mint," she would say, whenever Mia found herself trapped in the dark and scared. "Look around you. You're safe."

Mia faced Padraig once more...and the light switched on.

"Dumbledore was a wise man," she said when she could finally find her voice.

"Yeah. He was."

Padraig was still looking at her, and she felt a pull. Actually, she'd been feeling the pull for days, but she'd tried to ignore it. She was attracted to Padraig, and given the way he was looking at her now, she'd say the feeling was mutual.

Mia had spent the better part of last night tossing and turning in her hotel bed, debating the wisdom of acting on that attraction. Common sense and intelligence said no. For one thing, they were at the beginning of her dream vacation. And while Padraig insisted on playing her "forever" friend, there was still too much they didn't know about each other.

And then, of course, there was the fact that she was dying. It would be the height of cruelty to initiate something that could only end in heartbreak if the sexual tension evolved into deeper, much more genuine feelings than the friendship strings that were already tugging too tight.

"Mia," Padraig said.

"Yeah?"

"I'm going to kiss you."

"I don't think that's a good idea."

Padraig turned to face her, studying her expression closely. He'd told her that if there was ever a time to drop all pretense, to be true, it was now. She'd taken those words to heart. So she didn't bother to hide her desires.

"You want me to kiss you."

"Yeah. I do. But I'm afraid we both know how this story ends. There's no happy ending, Paddy."

His smile grew as he cupped her cheeks. "Call me that again."

His family's nickname for him had fallen out without thought. "Paddy," she whispered as he bent his head closer.

Padraig didn't halt until their lips were nearly touching. "You're wrong, Tilly Mint." It was all he said before his lips took hers.

If she'd been sitting at the pub and placing a bet on how Padraig would kiss, she would have lost every penny she had.

Her sweet, gentle friend was harboring a wild side. He didn't hold anything back as he took her mouth almost roughly. Their lips parted and his tongue touched hers, tantalizing her taste buds with the sweet soda he'd drunk earlier. Padraig gripped her cheeks firmly, using his hold to twist her head incrementally, moving her so he could deepen the kiss, claim more.

It wasn't her first kiss, but it sure as hell felt like it.

He pulled away, the two of them gasping for breath, but his hands never left her face.

"You're wrong," he repeated. Before she could ask about what, he answered. "We have no idea how this story is going to end."

She wanted to argue with him, but when she considered it, she realized he was right. They only knew one thing. She was going to die. But every single other thing was unwritten. The pen was in her hand.

"I don't want this to end sad."

"Then it won't," he said.

This time, when hope returned, it stuck.

"Okay," she whispered.

"Ready to go?"

She nodded.

The two of them walked out of the park, stopping to buy matching Thing 1 and Thing 2 shirts.

Padraig climbed into the back of the taxi after her, sliding close as he wrapped his arm around her shoulders. The polite distance they'd been maintaining had vanished with the kiss. She rested her head on his shoulder as his fingers skimmed along her thigh, gently caressing her skin.

Turning slightly, she placed her hand on his chest, mimicking the same suggestive, tantalizing stroking.

Padraig placed a soft kiss on her head, and the two of them rode in complete silence, letting their hands do all the talking.

Once they returned to the hotel, they took the elevator to their floor. They'd reserved two rooms, Padraig's across the hall from hers.

She dug her keycard from her pocket, noticing Padraig wasn't doing the same. She smiled at his almost wolfish demeanor. Her heart raced as she struggled to recall why she thought this was a bad idea. For the life of her, every answer felt more like an excuse than a reason.

So she let it all go.

"Paddy," she said as she opened the door. "I want—"

That was all she managed before she found herself inside the room, her back pressed up against the closed door, Padraig's lips on hers again.

If she'd thought the kiss at the park was hot, this one was downright combustible.

His hands roamed, touching everything as if he couldn't get enough of her. He gripped her hips, then dipped his hands beneath her shirt. She gasped, their lips parting briefly as his hands cupped and squeezed her breasts.

Mia felt the same need to explore. She tugged his T-shirt, clawing at it desperately in an attempt to take it off. Padraig stepped away from her for a split second to drag it over his head and toss it to the floor.

Her gaze drifted downwards, managing only a glimpse of his muscular and—holy shitballs—sexy chest before he was back, kissing her with more passion than she'd ever felt in her life.

Mia winced as a lightning bolt of pain struck her right between the eyes, her vision going black for a split second. Padraig didn't notice her distress, and she was grateful. She didn't want to stop. Didn't want this perfect day ruined by a fucking tumor. It was already taking too much away from her. She couldn't let it take this away too.

Padraig turned her toward the room, kissing her as he backed her up. Then he took care of her T-shirt, tossing it away before stepping back to look.

"Mia." He whispered her name with the same reverence some people evoked the name of their god. "You're so beautiful."

She tried to smile, but there was no more denying this wasn't going to end well. The throbbing pain was growing unbearable and flashing, floating lights were messing with her eyesight.

"Paddy," she said, her voice sounding faraway through the excruciating thudding in her ears.

Her tone must have been enough, because Padraig's entire demeanor changed. Her sexy lover vanished as the kind caretaker returned. He gently helped her lie down on the bed, covering her up with the sheet.

"Do you have something to take for the pain?"

"Bathroom," she replied weakly. A small cry escaped as the shooting pains escalated.

She'd pushed herself too far. What had she been thinking? Getting on an airplane? Spending a day walking around in bright sunshine? Riding those roller coasters?

"Light." She gestured toward the curtains. Fortunately, Padraig understood her request as he quickly pulled the room-darkening curtains shut, casting the room in blessed blackness.

She lay there, fighting the urge to scream when Padraig returned to her side again, this time with pills and a glass of water.

Mia lifted her head to take them, but the movement was too much, the pain so intense, a wave of nausea wafted through her.

"Fuck," she muttered, as she dashed from the bed to the bathroom, arriving not a second too soon as her stomach emptied. She placed her forehead against the cool porcelain of the toilet.

"It's okay." Padraig lifted her hair and placed a cold washcloth on the back on her neck.

"Please, go away. I don't want you to see—" Her request was cut short as she threw up again.

Padraig didn't leave. Instead, he sank down on the edge of the bathtub, continuing to hold her hair. "I'm not going anywhere, Mia, so don't ask."

Her whole body hurt. She trembled and cried as she continued to wretch. Her stomach was empty, but not giving up, clamping, convulsing as the pain in her head turned white-hot.

Padraig handed her a tissue and she realized her nose was bleeding.

"God," she gasped, hating every second of what was happening. "Please, Padraig. Leave."

He moved from his spot on the tub, kneeling next to her. He flushed the toilet, then took the tissue from her, applying pressure.

"It's going to be okay, Mia. We'll ride it out. Together."

"I'm disgusting," she said after a few minutes. The dry heaves had stopped and her nose no longer bled, but her head still pounded.

"You're beautiful."

She knew he was trying to be kind, but the words merely bounced off. "This was a mistake."

"Nope. It wasn't. Do you want another pill?"

The last one had ended up in the toilet along with her lunch. Even so, her stomach didn't feel steady enough for anything at the moment. "Vicious circle. Sick because of headache, but I can't take the pill to cure the headache because I'm sick."

"We'll wait half an hour and try again. Come on."

He stood, then helped her rise from the floor. Her legs were weak, so she reached for the sink for support.

Padraig took charge, lifting her and carrying her to the bedroom. It was the first time she could ever remember anyone carrying her in her entire life. Surely her grandma had carried her when she was a baby, but those memories were gone.

He placed her on the bed. "You want your pajamas on?"

It occurred to her belatedly that she was in nothing but her bra and shorts. She'd kicked off her flip-flops just before the pain hit.

"I...maybe you could just help me pull off my shorts. They feel sort of gross after a day at the amusement park."

Padraig was all business as he unhooked her shorts and tugged them off. If her head didn't still hurt so badly, she might have been mortified to have his first view of her nearly naked body be this one.

He drew the covers over her and she expected him to leave.

"I just need to sleep for a little while."

"I know." He walked to the other side of the bed and, to her surprise, he shed his own shoes and shorts before climbing under the covers next to her. "A nap will do us both some good."

"You don't have to—"

"Stop telling me to leave, Mia."

She fell silent, fighting not to cry again. Poor Padraig had seen too many of her tears as it was. "I'm sorry," she said at last, unable to shake the regret that she'd destroyed their perfect day.

"I think I'm going to have to make you a list of do's and don'ts. Number one is going to be don't apologize for things that aren't your fault."

A sob escaped. Her head and her body and her stomach...God, every part of her hurt.

But none of her ached more than her heart.

***

Padraig lay in the dark room, listening to Mia's quiet breathing as she slept. Every now and then she'd whimper, letting him know her head was still hurting.

His chest had been tight with anger ever since he'd seen her draped over the toilet, her body racked with pain. Simply knowing someone was sick, and seeing it up close and personal were two completely different things. Mia had seemed so healthy that he'd allowed himself to believe the ticking time bomb in her head wasn't poised to explode.

He wouldn't—couldn't—show her how much her illness was tearing him up. So instead, he'd lay here for the last two hours in the blackness, wide awake and cursing God.

No one deserved this. No one.

Mia was a good person, a sweet woman who'd suffered enough shit in her lifetime. There was no way to explain this, to offer him some answer that would make what she was going through okay.

He wanted to hit something, tear it apart with his bare hands.

For Mia, he'd play a role, be positive and optimistic, but that didn't mean he was fucking alright with this. Because he wasn't.

His phone pinged. Moving slowly, he sat up then reached down to grab his cell from the back pocket of his shorts.

The text was a question from Colm.

Good day?

His brother teased him about his pilgrimage to Harry Potter World, but Padraig suspected Colm was really jealous.

He typed out his reply.

Yeah.

His one word answer pulled the trigger and Colm's response was quick.

What's wrong?

Suddenly the timing of Colm's text didn't seem so coincidental. They joked from time to time about the twin link, but he suspected they tried to laugh it off because both of them were really freaked out about it.

There had been too many times in the past when they'd both had a sense that the other was in trouble.

She got sick. Bad headache. Shouldn't have done so much at theme park.

Padraig's response didn't come close to saying what he really felt.

How are you doing?

And apparently Colm knew it. He recalled Colm asking Mia for that dance, that he'd issued her some sort of warning in hopes of protecting him. Padraig hadn't called his brother out. There hadn't been time before they'd left for the airport.

Now...

He understood what his brother had been trying to do. How he'd hoped to save Padraig from this barrage of ugly emotions. The helplessness, the frustration and—God help him—the outright fury.

Padraig studied his brother's text for a full minute, uncertain how to reply.

His hesitance didn't go unnoticed.

Don't kill anybody, Colm warned. *Don't fancy spending months in Florida, defending you in court.*

Padraig couldn't muster a grin, unable to shake his frustration, so he texted what he felt.

It's not fair.

Now it was Colm's turn to take his time responding. When he did, Padraig was relieved his brother hadn't hit him with that fucking "life's not fair" adage. If he had, Padraig would have had to interrupt the vacation to fly home and beat the shit out of his twin.

Instead, his intelligent brother found the right words.

No. It's not fair. It's wrong on every level. But she needs you to make it okay. So make it okay, P. Make it tolerable. Hell, make it better than tolerable. Make every minute, every second count. It's the only way you can take something so unfair and say UP YOURS to the universe.

Up yours.

Yeah. He could do that.

The heaviness lifted.

Thanks, bro.

Colm sent him a thumbs-up emoticon, followed by, *Just remember this,* accompanied by the middle finger emoticon.

Padraig chuckled. He'd been itching for a fight, and Colm gave him the perfect punching bag.

Placing his phone on the nightstand, he rose and walked to the bathroom. Grabbing Mia's pain medicine and some water, Padraig returned to the bed.

She stirred when he sat down next to her, her eyes opening slowly.

"Head still hurt?" he asked quietly.

She nodded.

"Here." He lifted her head gently, helping her take the pills.

"Why are you being so nice to me?"

He bent down to place a kiss on her forehead. "Because you're easy to be nice to."

"That's not an answer. I was basically a stranger a few weeks ago."

Things had gotten too heavy since their return to the hotel room. Padraig didn't know how to answer so he reverted to humor, desperate to see her smile like she had when they rode on the Hogwarts Express.

He gave her a playful wink. "At first, it had a lot to do with karma. Mine's probably on shaky ground. Drink too much, gossip as much as my Pop Pop, cuss and gamble more than I should."

Mia picked up on the joke instantly, her sleepy grin emerging. "Oh, I see. So, helping the dying girl buys you good karma."

"Tons of it. Figure I can place wagers on every Super Bowl from here on out and embellish every sentence with as many 'fucks' and 'shits' as I want and I'll be in good standing."

"Glad to be able to help you out." Then something occurred to her as she added, "You said 'at first'. What's your reason for helping me now?"

Padraig gave her a quick, hard kiss on her smiling lips. "I want to get in your pants."

She barked out a loud laugh that obviously cost her, since she winced. "Don't make me laugh. My head hurts too bad."

"Sorry, Tilly Mint. I'll save my teasing for another time then."

She grasped his hand and lifted it to her lips, placing a sweet kiss on his knuckles. "Whatever your reason, I'm glad you're here."

"There's no place on earth I'd rather be, Mia. Not a single one."

Her eyes began to drift closed. "Paddy," she said, even as she rolled away from him, sleep claiming her fast.

"Hmm?"

"I think I'm going to fall in love with you."

She was asleep the second she finished speaking so she didn't see his face.

She missed the impact her words had on him.

Padraig's smile grew so big the stretch almost hurt his cheeks.

And his heart.

Jesus, what she'd done to his heart.

"I'm going to fall in love with you too," he whispered to the still room. Then he glanced across the room, flashing his middle finger toward the window and the universe beyond.

"Up yours."

Chapter Eight

April 22

Mia released a long, contented sigh.

"That's a happy sound," Padraig said from the lounger next to hers.

Mia didn't bother to open her closed eyes, the dark sunglasses muting the bright Florida sunshine. "What you're really saying is the sigh sounds better than my groaning and whining all day yesterday."

They'd been forced to cancel their trip to Epcot when Mia awoke the day after Universal with her headache still intact. The pain hadn't subsided until late afternoon. She'd tried to convince Padraig to go out and do something, hating that her health was ruining his vacation, but he'd remained by her side in the dark room, bringing her pills, forcing her to eat little bits of food, and telling her silly stories about his family by way of distraction. She'd suffered from intense headaches before, but yesterday's pain had seemed somewhat more bearable, thanks to Padraig.

Mercifully, they'd planned a relaxing day at Discovery Cove, and when she'd awoken this morning the pain in her head was gone, replaced by the mild soreness that told her the worst was over. For now.

Discovery Cove was an amazing place with a lazy river, aviary, pools with couches and, best of all, serve-yourself margarita machines.

They'd already taken a few leisurely floats along the river, tried their hand at snorkeling and now they were soaking up the rays. She and Padraig were going to stick out like sore thumbs when they returned to chilly Maryland. She looked forward to showing off her suntanned skin next to everyone's pasty winter white.

"Last day in Florida," Padraig said. "Everything you hoped it would be?"

She nodded. "Yeah. It's wonderful. I sort of thought Harry Potter World was going to be the highlight, but I think today might be winning."

"This place is pretty cool. Might want to try the snorkeling thing again before we leave. Liked looking at all those fish."

"I'm in. Later. After I finish this margarita."

"Drink away. Sort of hoping I get a taste of it myself later."

She glanced over and lifted her cup. "I didn't realize you wanted any. Help yourself."

He shook his head, his gaze drifting to her lips. "Not that way."

Mia felt her cheeks heat, less from the sun and more from something she didn't want to feel. "I don't think—"

"Later," he said. "For right now, I'm perfectly happy to just lay here and talk. Get to know you better."

"Get to know me?"

He nodded. "Yeah."

She snorted. "I'm an open book. And a boring one. I'd rather learn more about you."

"Like what?"

"Who was your first kiss?" she asked. The more she learned about Padraig, the more she wanted to know.

He chuckled. "Kelli."

"Seriously?" She'd gotten to know Padraig's female best friend a bit better over the past couple of weeks, and she genuinely liked the woman. Part of her wondered why Kelli and Padraig had chosen to remain friends rather than date. "And it didn't work out?"

Padraig shook his head. "No. I'm afraid she was a bit of a tramp. Kissed me for a quarter, then got fifty cents to give Tommy Martinson a kiss under the sliding board."

Mia rolled her eyes. "Elementary school?"

Padraig was pleased with his joke. "Fifth grade."

"Why don't we skip the schoolyard stories and bounce forward to the real ones?"

He chuckled. "Okay, but you're missing some great stuff from sixth grade."

"Still Kelli?"

"Nah. She told me I was a crappy kisser and moved on to other guys."

It was obvious Kelli hadn't kissed Padraig lately, because there was nothing crappy about his kissing. "So who was your first love?"

Padraig tilted his head. "If I tell you, are you going to tell me about yours?"

She nodded. "If you want. Though I'll warn you now. There's not much to tell."

"I'll be the judge of that. My first love was Stephanie Bell. She was a little blonde cheerleader on the junior varsity squad, and she definitely knew how to fill out that uniform."

Mia snorted. "Great standards."

"Horny teenage boy standards. Believe me, they don't run much deeper than that in high school."

"And this was your first great love?"

Padraig shrugged. "I thought she was. We made out about a dozen times. And I fell head over heels when she let me touch what was under that cheer sweater."

"Let me guess. She broke your heart."

He nodded. "Got a better offer. Quarterback on the football team asked her out."

She sat up on the lounger and gave him a quick up and down. "You're a big guy. Surprised *you* didn't play football."

"I did, but I was on special teams. Nowhere near the same social status as the quarterback."

"And you were devastated?"

"Completely. Until Jillian Barker caught my eye."

"She had big boobs too?"

He shook his head, grinning like the Cheshire cat. "Nope. But she had this sweet little ass that looked pretty amazing in her volleyball shorts."

Mia lifted her sunglasses as the sun peeked behind a fluffy white cloud. "Any relationships based on silly stuff like emotions or, I don't know, personality over appearance?"

Padraig sat up and faced her. He'd tossed his sunglasses on top of a towel on the sand next to the chair earlier, and she was glad. She liked having an unobstructed view of his expressive brown eyes. Right now, he was clearly having a good time at her expense, teasing her rather than giving her straight answers.

"Oh, you mean true love, not superficial."

She squeezed her water bottle, shooting him squarely in the middle of his muscular bare chest.

"Hey, that's cold!" he said, wiping away the wetness with the T-shirt he'd been using as a pillow.

Padraig had caught her looking at his too-sexy-for-her-sanity body too many times today. Of course, she figured they were even, because he hadn't even tried to sneak a peek at Mia in her one-piece, opting instead for the straight eyebrow-waggling ogle accompanied by a wolf whistle.

The swimsuit was a little lower cut than she usually went for, but she'd decided what the hell. The shopping excursion for the trip had been Padraig's cousin Yvonne's idea. And Yvonne had promised Mia that Padraig's eyes would bug out of his head if he saw her in this swimsuit.

At the time, Mia had assured Yvonne that wasn't something she was trying to do. And this morning, when she'd donned it, she had still felt that way. Her headache had come at the perfect time, reminding Mia why pursuing anything beyond friendship with Padraig was a bad idea.

"True love, huh?" Padraig leaned forward, his elbows resting on his knees. "That would be Allyson Murray."

"Still in high school?"

He shook his head. "Nope. Met her two years after graduation. She waits tables at one of the local seafood places. Or at least, she did. To tell you the truth, I'm not sure what she's doing now. We dated for a year and a half, and I'm not going to lie, I thought she was the one."

"What happened?"

"An old boyfriend hopped back on the scene. He'd graduated from college with his fancy business administration degree, and apparently that looked like a better future to her than a guy waiting tables in his family's pub."

"Seems like a silly reason to break up with someone if you're in love."

He shrugged. "You're right. Once I stopped drowning my sorrows after she dumped me, I put two and two together and figured out my feelings were more engaged than hers. Sort of made it easier for me to move on."

"Anyone else since then?"

"A few, but none of them stuck for one reason or another. One woman cheated on me. Another got a better job in New York and neither of us was ready to take it to the next level to stay together. Life takes funny turns sometimes. I think if Jenny hadn't gotten that job in New York, she and I might have made it to the altar. But the job came too soon in the relationship and that was that."

"Yeah. Funny turns." Or unfunny turns, she thought, though she didn't say it. She'd say her life had missed the turn and she was currently taking a Thelma-and-Louise style nosedive off the cliff.

"Okay. Your turn. First love."

She grinned. "Schoolyard or serious."

"Surprise me."

Mia glanced toward the water, wondering where to begin. Her past relationships, though fewer and less serious, sounded a lot like Padraig's. People meeting and connecting at the wrong time.

"I dated a lot of guys in high school. But none of them were serious boyfriends, and while we made out and stuff, I actually didn't lose my virginity to any of them. At the time, my primary objective in life was to piss my mother off. So I'd bring these guys home, we'd make out on the couch, she'd get home from work and lose her shit. Always screaming that if I got knocked up, she'd make me get an abortion because there was no way she was raising another unwanted kid."

Padraig's smile turned to a scowl, and Mia realized she hadn't really meant to reveal that. She'd never told anyone about her mother's cruelty. Or the things she'd done to provoke it. She and her mother had always had a caustic relationship. When she was younger, it was easy to blame her mother for all the hate, but now, Mia could see she hadn't done anything to help the situation. Most times she went out of her way to make everything worse.

"I hope I never meet your mom," Padraig said darkly. "I'm not sure what I'd say to her, but I promise you it wouldn't be nice."

"You'll never meet her." She sighed and decided to get them back on track, move the conversation back to safer topics. "My first love was named Laurence. He was the manager of his dad's ice cream store at the mall where I had a part-time job. We dated my whole senior year. He was twenty-one and had his own place. I was sleeping on a couch at my friend's house, so a couple, three times a week, I'd spend the night at his place. My friend's family was perfectly nice, but there was always this underlying atmosphere that told me I was imposing. So, I tried to stay out of the house as much as possible so I wouldn't bother them or wear out my welcome."

"Was Laurence a good guy?"

"I thought he was. At first. I was actually crazy about him. He was cute and charming and he swept me off my feet."

"You said at first. What happened later?"

"Shortly after I graduated from high school, I suggested that maybe I should move in with him. He laughed and said that his other girlfriends wouldn't like that."

"What a prick!"

Mia laughed, loving Padraig's heated response. "Yep. He was a total dick."

"Please tell me there were some nicer guys in your past."

"Just one. Mark. And he and I split for the same reason you and Jenny did. I got the job here in

Baltimore and we just didn't see a future together. Didn't mean he wasn't a great guy. We had a lot of fun together. It just wasn't going to be anything more than dating."

Mia wiped her brow, hot from lying in the sun so long. "Should we do the lazy river again? Cool off?"

Padraig nodded, taking her hand to help her up. However, he used that grip to tug her closer. Wrapping his arms around her, her breasts pressed against his chest, he lowered his head, intent on kissing her.

Mia pushed back, her retreat stopping him.

"Mia—"

"Please, Paddy. I don't think we should kiss anymore."

His frown grew. "Why not?"

She blew out a long, sad sigh. "Because I don't want to hurt you."

Padraig's voice was deep with something that sounded a lot like anger. "How are you hurting me?"

"Don't make me say it. Don't make me spell it out."

He released his grip on her, his expression a mix of frustrated and sad. "I know what I'm doing, Mia."

She dug deep, determined to hold to her resolve. The headache helped ground her, helped her remember why starting a relationship was wrong. She was going to die. Which meant Padraig would be left behind to deal with the aftermath. If they continued to grow close, her name would be added to the list of women who'd broken his heart in the past. She didn't want to do that to him. There was precious little she could control in her life at the moment. But *this* she could. "Let me do the right thing."

"This isn't the right thing."

She put her sunglasses back on, not because of the brightness, but because she hoped it would hide the tears she was trying not to shed. "I think it is."

"Dammit, Mia," he said loudly. "I care about you. God, I'm attracted to you. You're everything I've been looking for in a woman."

"Including the tumor?" It was a snarky, shitty thing to say, and she regretted it the instant it flew out.

"Don't," he said through clenched teeth. "Don't do that."

She turned away from him, watching the families, parents with their kids, laughing as they reached for noodles, racing toward the cave that served as an entrance to the lazy river. Padraig was made to be a husband and a father. She couldn't give him that. "Happily ever after isn't in the cards for me."

"I don't believe that."

She gave him an incredulous glare. "You see this ending well?"

"I don't think there's a certain time limit you have to hit before you can use the words 'happily ever after.' You're defining it all wrong. You seem to think a happy ending only comes after years and years of being with someone. My grandma Sunday died in her forties. Do you think if my Pop Pop had known the ending, he would have walked away from her, thrown away what they shared, what they felt for each other, simply because he was going to live fifty years longer than her?"

Mia stopped trying to hold back the tears. "Of course not," she whispered.

She had only had a handful of conversations with Pop Pop, and he'd mentioned his beloved Sunday in nearly all of them, quoting something she always used to say, or pointing out how one of his kids or grandkids was like her. Mia had always assumed Sunday had died an old woman, that her death had been more recent.

To find out she'd died so young...

Mia wasn't sure what to do with that fact.

"No one gets guarantees in life, Mia. I could walk out of this park and get hit by a car. *Boom.* It's not the end that matters. It's the life you live *before* the end. I'm not walking away from you, from us, simply because we know the ending beforehand. You know, in some ways you can look at that as a curse, but in others, it might be a blessing. You're not taking anything for granted like the rest of us, who just keep marching around aimlessly like we've got all the time in the world. You have the chance to make your days count. And not just some of them. All of them."

She swiped the tears, swiping the back of her hand under her runny nose. "That's just it, Paddy! I have *days.* You have years. Why would you sign on for certain heartbreak?"

"Heartbreak comes after love. If you want the love, you have to risk the hurt. I'm not afraid, Mia."

Mia bit her lower lip, struggling to stem the tears. She still wasn't willing to give in, but he'd punched a hell of a hole into her resolve.

"Mia," he whispered, turning her toward him. She didn't resist the soft kiss he gave her, but she didn't move to deepen it and she didn't reach out to touch him, even though she desperately wanted to.

He sighed as he pulled away. "Will you promise to at least consider what I've said?"

She nodded, her throat too constricted to speak.

"Good." He took her hand and tugged her toward the edge of the water. "Come on. We're not screwing up any of our days in Florida. We're here to have fun, and that's what we're going to do."

Mia pushed her fears deep inside, desperate to give Padraig the vacation he deserved. He was right. They'd lost too much time to her illness. Hell, even when her head didn't hurt, she was letting it impact things.

Enough.

She'd promised to consider what he'd said. She wasn't sure how she'd be able *not* to. Everything he said was beautiful, sweet, comforting.

And terrifying.

Chapter Nine

April 25

Padraig stood outside the Musée d'Orsay and gave a fake groan. He'd been teasing Mia about his reluctance to spend a day at a museum ever since they'd begun preparations for their trip.

They'd spent the better part of the day before yesterday traveling, leaving Orlando in the afternoon, enduring a brief layover in Miami, then flying overnight to Paris. Rather than stay in a hotel, they'd rented an apartment for their four days in the City of Light.

Neither of them had managed to sleep much on the flight, something they'd considered when planning their Parisian excursions. They'd remained close to the apartment yesterday, napping until late afternoon, then heading to a local French restaurant for dinner.

Today was the beginning of their true Paris adventure. And they were here, Padraig sighed dramatically, at an art museum.

Mia rolled her eyes at him. "You know, a little culture wouldn't hurt you."

"You realize France is known for wine. I say we do a couple of wine tastings, get tipsy and make out in front of the Eiffel Tower."

"Come on." She grabbed his hand and tugged him up the stairs to the entrance.

He hadn't tried to kiss her since their talk at Discovery Cove. He'd told Mia how he felt, what he wanted. Ultimately, the decision was hers. He certainly wouldn't force her into something she didn't want.

The problem was, he could tell she wanted him as much as he wanted her. She was denying them the chance to take things to the next level because she felt like it was her job to protect his feelings. While he respected her for the attempt, it also frustrated the hell out of him.

They entered the museum, and Padraig was instantly taken aback by the size and sheer grandeur of the building.

"Whoa."

She smiled at him, clearly pleased that he was as overwhelmed as she was. "It's even better than the pictures online," she said softly.

They grabbed a map, then started walking along the grand entryway.

The massive foyer was lined with huge marble statues. Padraig leaned down and whispered, "You didn't tell me there was nudie art. I wouldn't have complained so much."

Mia giggled. "You're terrible. Behave yourself."

They stopped to look at anything that caught their eye. He was surprised to discover how much Mia knew about art.

"I took an art appreciation class online. It was the only course I took that didn't have a darn thing to do with my associate's degree. I found so much of it fascinating."

They walked into one of the galleries and Padraig meandered over to where a large group of people stood, taking photos of a painting. Stepping closer, he read the plaque on the wall and his eyes widened.

Mia caught up, stopping next to him. "What is it?"

"Van Gogh," he said reverently. "It's a van Gogh."

"Oh, I remember studying this in my class. It's a painting of his actual bedroom."

"I can't believe I'm standing in front of an honest-to-God van Gogh painting."

Mia clasped hands with him, squeezing his. "You made fun, but you're an art fan too."

"I didn't think I was until this moment. I didn't expect to be so..." He struggled to find a word to describe his sudden rush of emotion. "Excited. Moved."

"And we haven't even made our way to the top floor where the rest of the Impressionists are yet. I bet those paintings knock your socks off."

"Show me," he said, allowing her to lead the way. They climbed the stairs, making their way to the exhibit that had drawn Mia to the museum to begin with. He'd originally questioned her desire to come to the Musée d'Orsay, as opposed to the more popular Louvre across the river.

Her answer had been Renoir.

Padraig had Googled the artist that night, and he began to understand.

"Wow," Mia whispered as they entered the large room that housed the paintings of so many famous Impressionists, artists even he'd heard of despite not being a fan of the medium—Monet, Manet, Cézanne, and Degas.

"It's a Mary Cassatt." Mia stopped before a large painting of a girl sitting in a garden. "I love the colors of this. Did you know she was a friend of Degas?"

He shook his head. "Nope. I'm basically a blank slate here."

She grinned. "That's kind of what's great about art. You don't have to know anything about the artist or the painting. You can simply look at the artwork and decide how it makes you feel."

Padraig looked back at the Cassatt painting. "Wonder what she's sewing so intently."

Mia shrugged. "I don't know, but I wouldn't mind spending some time, sitting in the midst of all those flowers. I could do without that long dress though."

They continued walking until they stopped before Degas's "The Ballet Class."

"It's just incredible, isn't it? So many of these paintings were created in the late eighteen-hundreds. To think that something so beautiful could survive a Great Depression, revolutions, wars."

"Did you ever take a ballet class?" Padraig asked when Mia continued to linger, studying the painting.

She shook her head. "No, but my best friend in middle school was in ballet. My grandma and I went to watch her in a recital once, just a few months before my grandmother died. Grandma said she'd sign me up for dance class the next fall, but it never happened. She got sick, and then…"

She didn't finish her comment. She didn't have to. It was clear the painting evoked a memory that made her sad. As he looked around the room, Padraig studied the faces of the visitors rather than the artwork, and he understood. The expressions of the other patrons reflected so many different emotions, from wonder and awe to sadness to joy.

It was time to find a new emotion for Mia. She'd been knee-deep in sadness for too long.

Padraig glanced around and spotted something familiar from his internet search. The perfect distraction. "Hey, isn't that a Renoir?"

Mia's eyes widened with excitement as she turned to look. "It is."

They wandered along, taking in her favorite artist's work. She knew a lot of information about each piece that she shared with him. He noticed that many of Renoir's works were portraits of people who'd lived during the artist's time, and those were the ones Mia studied the longest.

When they reached the portrait of a young girl in a white blouse, Mia whispered, "Oh!"

"A favorite?" he asked.

She shook her head. "I've actually never seen this one. She's beautiful."

Padraig studied the dark-haired girl and agreed that Renoir had captured her very well, from her wispy black hair to her rosy cheeks to the lace on her blouse.

He looked at the nameplate next to the painting and attempted in very poor French to read the name of the painting. "Jeune fille assise. Helene Bellon, c. 1909."

Mia giggled at his terrible pronunciation, but didn't bother to correct him. Probably because her French was just as bad. They decided their first night in the city that they would have been smarter to try to learn at least a few French words before traveling to Paris. As it was, they were two lost souls with three years of high school Spanish between them and no more than half a dozen French words in their arsenal.

Last night at dinner, they'd merely pointed to things on the menu and hoped for the best. It had made the dining experience an adventure to say the least, considering they didn't have a clue what they were getting.

"I love this portrait." She turned back to the painting and he tilted his head, looking at it closer, trying to figure out what it was about this one that spoke to her.

"Why?"

"It's her eyes. God, they say everything, don't they?"

"She looks sad to me," Padraig said after trying to read the young girl's expression.

"Does she? Wow. That's funny. I don't see that. I mean, I think she looks like she's seen something sad or had to deal with something hard. Yet she looks undefeated to me, even powerful. Like she knows her worth even if those around her don't."

Padraig didn't see any of that, but for some reason this woman who'd lived over a hundred years ago spoke to Mia. She seemed to have discovered a kindred spirit in the ghost of Helene, preserved in oil paint.

They stood in silence a few minutes longer. Mia continued to stare at the painting, but Padraig was more interested in the living, breathing embodiment of the portrait who was standing next to him.

She shook herself out of her reverie slowly. When she turned to look at him, her smile was huge, genuine. "Trip made. This museum..." She couldn't find the words to express her happiness, but Padraig could see it, could read it in her eyes.

He also couldn't resist any longer. He'd kept a proper distance for two days, but his willpower was gone.

He was falling head over heels for Mia Curtis.

Leaning down, he kissed her. Their lips lingered, but he didn't miss the fact that she was kissing him back. In fact, her tongue darted out briefly to swipe across his lower lip.

He pulled back briefly. "Finished fighting this?"

She nodded without hesitation. "I want…" Her words faded again.

"I want it too," he said.

Mia glanced back at the portrait one last time. "I can't let this defeat me. It's going to kill me, but it's not going to defeat me."

"You're right. It's not. You're too powerful."

They spent two more hours in the museum, discussing the artwork and enjoying the amazing view of the city through one of two huge fifth-floor clocks.

Afterwards, they found a small café for lunch en route to the Eiffel Tower. They'd discussed going up, but Mia was afraid the height might trigger a headache, so they opted for taking countless photos below.

Their day wound down with a slow, scenic boat ride down the Seine River.

With each passing hour, their desire for each other grew to almost painful heights. Now that Mia had turned the corner, they'd let go of their inhibitions, spending the day holding hands, kissing and cuddling, while whispering sweet nothings and sexual innuendoes in each other's ears.

Padraig had spent the majority of their boat ride adjusting his pants to try to hide the hard-on that wouldn't go away, no matter how many math problems he solved in his head.

"Dinner at the apartment?" he asked, praying she wouldn't insist on going to a restaurant. There was no way he could sit through an entire meal and keep his hands off her.

"There's no food there." She looked as frustrated as he felt. Then her eyes brightened. "There! There's a small store. Let's grab some bread and cheese and wine and make a meal of that."

Padraig was halfway across the street by the time she'd finished her list. "Perfect."

They found everything she'd suggested, as wei some strawberries and grapes, and headed back to the apartment. As soon as they placed their bags of food on the kitchen counter, Padraig reached for her.

Pressing her against the cabinets, he gave her the kind of kiss he'd been wanting to give her since the museum. His lips pushed hers open and their tongues touched, explored. Mia's hands had found their way to his hair and she gripped it roughly, desperate to keep his mouth on hers.

Padraig wanted more. Tugging her blouse free from her pants, he reached beneath, cupping her breasts as she moaned into his mouth. Wrapping his hands around, he unsnapped her bra with a skill he hoped she didn't notice.

With the lace free, he was able to touch her breasts with nothing in the way. Her nipples were hard and…

"God." He pushed away from her, leaning on the counter behind him. The kitchen in the apartment was small so there weren't more than a few feet between them. "Unbutton that blouse, Mia, before I rip it off you."

"Whoa," she said, her fingers flying to the buttons on her shirt. "I've always thought that was kind of corny when a guy says it in a movie, but damn…I stand corrected."

"Lose the bra too," he said, torn between laughing and snarling about how long it was taking her.

"Yeah. About that bra. You know your way around the clasps, don't you?"

"High school, remember? I might not have book smarts, but that doesn't mean I'm not a quick learner."

She tugged her blouse over her shoulders, letting it fall to the floor. Her bra still covered her, held in place by one of her hands. Her cheeks were flushed, the way

125

they'd been when he'd introduced her to Sky and Teagan. He'd found Mia's shyness endearing that night.

Tonight...there was no room for it.

"Drop the bra, Mia."

She licked her lips nervously. "What about you?"

He drew his T-shirt over his head in one quick pull, tossing it to the floor.

"Oh. Wow." Her admiring gaze traveled the length of his torso.

"Bra. I'm not going to ask again."

Her eyes flew back to his. His dark tone aroused her as much as it fed her nervousness. However, it didn't take his brave woman long to find her nerve. She loosened her grip and let the bra fall off. Rather than cover herself with her hands, she stiffened her spine and lifted her chin, letting him look his fill.

He didn't fool himself into believing it was easy for her to hold that pose, to stand there so exposed. "Maybe it's time you realized your worth, Mia." He stepped closer, drawing his fingers over the top of one of her breasts, letting them drop lower to her nipple. He closed his thumb and forefinger around it and squeezed.

She gasped at the pressure.

"You're the most beautiful woman I've ever seen."

Mia was right. So many times today at the museum, she'd remarked on the eyes of the people portrayed in the paintings. Said she could see so much just by studying the eyes.

As he looked at hers, he felt as if he could read every emotion flowing through her at the moment. The fear, the hope, the longing, the passion. She was everything he'd ever wanted in a woman. Everything.

Cupping her cheeks with his hands, he resumed the kiss, taking her mouth harder than before. He was starving for her, hungry—no, ravenous—and ready to claim it all.

Her heart, her body, her soul.

Her future.

He would take every second she had left, and then he'd fight God, the universe, the doctors, whoever he had to, to steal even more.

She was his. And she would be until the day she took her last breath.

Mia cried out when he nipped at her lip, and he forced himself to take a step away. Both of them were breathing heavily, staring at each other, sizing the other up.

"Bedroom?" she asked, breathlessly.

He nodded.

The two of them made their way to her room and Padraig struggled to regain some semblance of control.

Mia stopped just short of the bed, turning to look at him.

"How long has it been?" he asked.

"One time maybe six, seven months ago. Before that…it had been a while."

Padraig absorbed that information, aware that her sexual experiences were limited. He wasn't exactly a player himself, but he had some definite needs that might scare her a bit.

He reached for the button on her shorts, unfastening it before tugging them and her panties off. "Lay down on the bed." He tried to temper the request, but as always, it came out more like a demand.

One that Mia responded to without question. Which didn't help his control at all.

He placed one knee beside her hip on the mattress, one hand by her head. Leaning over her, he ran his fingers along her body, feasting on her with not only his gaze, but with his touch as well.

Mia shivered each time he stroked a sensitive spot, and her cheeks grew pinker under his concentrated attention.

She jerked roughly when he pressed the tip of his index finger against her clit. Just one touch.

"Sorry," she whispered. "I'm so…"

"Ready?" he supplied.

She nodded, though he didn't need her answer. Mia was wet and hot and…yeah…ready.

"Open your legs." This time he didn't bother to soften his tone. Once more Mia complied, even though he knew she was slightly uncomfortable with the added exposure.

He drew his fingers along the slit between her legs. Her eyes closed as her breathing increased. She tried to hold back her soft cries, but Padraig didn't want her quiet. He wanted to hear everything. See everything. Feel everything.

He pressed two fingers inside her, relishing the way Mia thrust her hips upwards, fighting for more.

He stroked inside her half a dozen times, curling his fingers, seeking the hot spots. She didn't fail to let him know when he'd struck gold. Her cries grew louder and her hips gyrated faster, wilder.

She would come like this if he'd let her.

Instead, he pushed her to the brink, then tugged his fingers free.

Mia's eyes flew open and her forehead creased in confusion. She truly had been lost to the sensations.

"You're beautiful," he said. He would never get tired of telling her that, because it would never stop being true. Every single day he found something else beautiful about her. From the way she tried to hide her smile behind her hand, to the way she sounded when he drove his fingers deep inside her.

She reached up, her hands gripping his upper arms, alternating between caressing his muscles and squeezing them. She was a patient lover, one who didn't make demands. He wasn't used to that. Most women he knew would have pitched a fit if he'd left them hanging the way he just had Mia.

However, she seemed to appreciate his desire to draw this out. To make the moment last. To make it special.

"Can I touch you?" she whispered.

He rose, shedding his shorts and boxers before returning to the same position.

Mia looked down, her shyness vanishing, replaced instead by curiosity and desire. She slid her hand along his chest, not stopping until the head of his cock brushed against her knuckles.

"Wrap your hand around me, Mia. Squeeze it tight. Let me feel how good it's going to be when I slide inside you."

Her breathing, which had been rapid until that moment, appeared to seize, to stick in her chest. Neither of them sucked in a bit of air until her hand clasped around his dick and tightened.

Padraig placed his hand over hers, adding even more force to the grasp. Then he moved on to friction, drawing her palm up and down his hard flesh, showing her exactly what he liked.

Mia was a quick study. When she licked her lips, he bent down to touch the new wetness, to taste her again. She didn't release him, didn't slow her pace, even as he made love to her mouth, thrusting inside deeply, roughly.

Padraig let her push him to that same brink before pulling out of reach of her hand. For the first time, Mia started to protest.

"No." It was all he said. It was enough.

Mia fell silent, waiting for his next move. The alpha inside him roared.

Moving down, he lifted her legs, placing her knees on his shoulders as he pressed his mouth to her clit.

Her hands flew to his head, pushing and pulling with equal measure.

"Paddy, I…"

He lifted his head briefly, forcing her gaze to meet his. "I'm not stopping, so stop trying to push me away."

Her fingers relaxed in his hair, her resistance melting in an instant.

"No one has ever…"

Padraig heard her words and mentally shook his head. He was perfectly aware that there were a lot of guys out there who wouldn't go down on a woman. Leave it to Mia to find only that type.

He ran his tongue along her slit before pressing it inside her. He thrust in and out, enjoying her soft mewls of delight and surprise. He'd told her once she was easy to be nice to. That wasn't a lie.

Mia didn't make demands or have a selfish bone in her body.

This time he was ready to take her all the way, but it was Mia who pulled away just before her climax struck.

"I want you inside me."

He tilted his head and gave her a grin. "That's definitely where we're headed, Mia. I want you to come first."

She shook her head. "I want it to be with you. Together."

Padraig moved upwards, caging her beneath him to kiss her once more. "You realize you can have more than one, right?"

She giggled. "I've heard rumors of that strange magic, though I've never experienced it. Even so, I want our first time to be you *and* me."

He nodded, deciding her request was exactly what he wanted to. "Let me grab a condom." He started to reach for his shorts, but she stopped him.

"I'm on birth control. When the headaches first started, my doctor thought it might be hormonal."

"Mia..." He hesitated. Not because he didn't want to take her with nothing between them, but because he wanted her to be sure.

"Please."

There was nothing he would deny her. And it had nothing to do with her health. It had everything to do with the fact that she had his heart in her teeth. Pop Pop had warned him, told him he'd fall fast and hard.

Truer words were never spoken.

Padraig kissed her again. Her legs parted, allowing him to lay atop her, his weight supported by his elbows. His cock rested against her slit, enveloping him in her incredible heat.

Neither of them moved to the next part. Content to drag this kiss, this night out forever.

After several minutes, her hips began to tilt, just a little bit. But it was enough to send the "do it now" message from his dick to his brain.

"God, Mia. I want you so badly."

She smiled. "I'm yours."

He lifted his hips, pressing the head of his cock against her opening. Their gazes held as he slowly slid inside.

Once he was fully lodged, he kissed her again.

"I'm trying to be gentle," he admitted, though the effort was costing him dearly.

She frowned. "Did I ask for gentle? I was sort of hoping for something that matched the 'I'm going to rip your blouse off' level."

He chuckled. "You might want to be careful what you wish for."

"Paddy," she said.

"Yeah?"

"If you're not able to do it, I don't mind taking control."

It was the perfect taunt. Revealing that she understood exactly what sort of impact it would have on him.

He shook his head, though his wolfish grin grew. "Oh man. I wish you hadn't said that."

"I regret nothing."

He hoped she felt that way after.

Until then...

Padraig pulled out until only the head of his cock remained inside, and then he thrust back in forcefully.

Unlike his first easy slide in, this motion packed a punch.

And it opened his eyes to something he hadn't noticed until that moment.

Mia preferred his roughness.

Her nails scored into his back, making a mark he'd feel for a few days, and her legs wrapped around his waist, squeezing him like a vise. The new position opened her more, allowed him to go deeper. He took full advantage.

Padraig began to thrust, driving into her with the speed and power he craved. Mia met him blow for blow, her cries turning to pleas for more.

"Harder. God, please, Paddy."

He gave her what she wanted. It still wasn't enough. He withdrew and flipped her facedown, dragging her hips toward him as he pounded back inside.

Mia's hands clenched into the duvet as she moved in unison with him, adding her own force. Padraig grasped a handful of her strawberry-blonde hair, using the grip to pull her back against his chest. With his free hand, he reached around to cup her breast. He squeezed the soft flesh, pinched her nipple.

Mia bent her head to one side, baring her neck to him, inviting him to kiss, to suck, to bite.

She wasn't idle, digging her nails into his thighs briefly before dragging them farther back to grip his ass. She tightened her hands, clenching his ass cheeks with the same pressure he was applying to her breasts.

Still he thrust inside. Still she met him, silently demanding even more.

"Mia," he cried out when his climax was imminent. "I'm there. I—"

He stroked her clit, desperate to make sure he gave her what she wanted.

Together.

Padraig thrust three more times, shallower, as the intensity became too much. Lightning flashed behind his closed eyelids.

Mia pulled from his grasp, dropping to her elbows, her head pressed to the mattress as she trembled through her own orgasm.

Her inner muscles clenched, milking every drop of come from him.

Padraig struggled to catch a deep breath, feeling as if he'd run a marathon.

Slowly, somewhat stiffly, Mia moved forward, separating them as she lay prone.

He longed to see her face.

"Roll over, Mia."

She did so, limp as a rag doll.

His smile provoked a scowl on her face. "You did this to me. I have no bones left in my body."

Padraig dropped next to her on the bed, running a single finger along her shoulder and arm. "Do you think a very Parisian-style dinner in bed might help restore your strength?"

"Dinner in bed? Really?" She began to push up excitedly, but Padraig pressed her down.

"Stay there. I'll make it."

For the first time since they'd entered the bedroom, Mia failed to follow a command. Probably because they were back to regular old Paddy and Mia, their sexual appetites sated for the time being.

She sat up the same time he did. However, before he could leave the bed, she crawled closer to him, giving him a kiss. "Do you think we can do that again later?"

He laughed. "The better question is, do you think we're going to make it out of this bed to see the rest of Paris?"

She grinned. "I wouldn't mind." Then her stomach growled, reminding him it had been hours since they last ate. His own hunger was starting to make itself known as well.

"Stay put," he said again, more firmly. "I'm making you dinner in bed."

"Okay." She moved to pull down the messed-up bedding, propping herself up in a seated position with the pillows against the headboard.

Padraig caught himself humming as he sliced off several chunks of cheese to put on a platter he'd found in one of the cabinets. He washed the grapes and strawberries and tossed the whole loaf of bread on, deciding they could rip off pieces to feed each other.

Then he opened a bottle of rosé, placed two wineglasses and the bottle of wine on the tray, and carried the overladen thing to the bedroom.

Mia had turned on the bedside lamps, and he noticed late afternoon had given way to evening. They relived their day as they ate and then turned off the lights, falling into each other's arms again.

The second time, he was able to give her gentle. They kissed and tickled and moved slowly, but at the end, the climax was just as powerful, just as earth-shattering.

He'd found her. His one true love.

And the clock was ticking.

Chapter Ten

April 26

Mia stood near a window in the funicular, watching as they rose higher and higher above the city. Today's plan was to see Sacré-Coeur and explore Montmartre. They'd added the tourist spot after seeing images of it on a travel site online. It looked exactly like Mia's idea of Paris. Romance and beauty.

She couldn't wait to reach the top, peering anxiously through the trees to try to catch a glimpse of the cathedral. Trees were obscuring some of the view, but as they continued to rise, she was impressed to see more and more of the town below.

Padraig stood next to her. However, he was looking at *her* rather than the passing scenery.

She smiled while keeping her eyes glued to what was outside. "You know you're missing a lot," she warned, letting him know she was aware of his staring.

Last night had been incredible. It had been so long since she'd fallen asleep in a man's arms. And even then...well...nothing she'd ever experienced came close to how she felt wrapped up in Padraig's strong embrace. While he was considerably larger than her, that size never intimidated. Instead, she felt sheltered, safe.

Mia had spent the years since her grandmother's death protecting herself. She had always believed her independence made her strong. She could see now all it had done was leave her lonely.

She'd wallowed in that state for so long, she hadn't even realized that was what it was. She hadn't felt alone since the night Padraig had followed her out of the pub. In the course of a single day, she'd discovered the worst and best things in her life.

"I'm not missing a damn thing." Padraig placed his hand on her waist and tugged her closer, nuzzling her cheek with his nose. He hadn't shaved since they'd left the States, claiming it was his "God-given duty as a Caps fan" to let the beard grow until they got knocked out of the Stanley Cup playoffs. While she wasn't a fan of the Caps, she was a huge fan of the beard, so for the first time in her life, she was rooting against her beloved Blackhawks.

Since waking up this morning, Padraig had managed to touch her no less than a million times. Sweet kisses, silly tickles, hair ruffles, hand-holding.

The funicular reached the top, reminding Mia that she'd missed the last half of the view outside as well. At this rate, she and Padraig would have been better served staying in bed.

"Behave," she warned him when his hand slipped from her lower back to her ass. "You're distracting me from Paris."

He laughed and clasped their hands, leading her from the funicular. "Come on. Let's see this cathedral of yours."

As they rounded the small path that led to Sacré-Coeur, the soft sounds of music caught her attention.

Once they reached the top, the world opened up in wondrous splendor. All of Paris lie beneath them, buildings seemingly stacked on top of each other, touching every square inch of the landscape. It was an array of colors and shapes and bright sunlight as far as the eye could see.

That was when Mia realized the music was still playing. A street musician sat several feet away playing an honest-to-God harp. Mia had never heard anything more beautiful.

"The *Titanic* song?" Padraig asked.

She nodded. "'My Heart Will Go On'."

He wrapped his arms around her waist, his cheek pressed against the side of her head, very much like Leo did with Kate in the movie, and together they took it all in.

Words weren't necessary. The place said everything.

Mia didn't bother to stem her tears. After weeks of crying in sorrow, today she was crying with utter joy.

Minutes passed as they soaked up the magic of it— the harp, the song, the cityscape, the sunshine.

They didn't stir until the last strains of the song faded.

Padraig whispered in her ear. "I think we found our song."

She smiled, swallowing deeply to lodge the lump forming there. "This is the most perfect moment of my life. If I could freeze time, it would be right now. Right here. With you."

Padraig kissed her cheek, not mentioning the wetness he found there. She turned to face him, giving him a much more meaningful kiss, trying to prove to him how much all of this truly meant to her.

Padraig cupped her cheeks as they parted, pressing his forehead against hers. "If I was freezing time, it would have been last night. Watching you sleep."

He gave her a soft kiss on the cheek before leaning closer to whisper, "After I rocked your world."

She laughed as he pulled away and gave her a mischievous wink. Only Padraig could take a happy moment and make it even better. Finding a way to add laughter to the joy.

"I love you."

The words came out without thought, without regard to the fact they hadn't been spoken before. She didn't care. She felt it. And she wasn't going to hide anything from him. Life was too short to play games, even without a brain tumor.

"I love you too, Mia. So much it hurts."

She understood that sentiment. Even now, her heart ached at the thought of leaving. Not just Paris, but...life.

It was a cruel irony that she'd found forever at the end.

Mia pushed the thought away before it could even land. Her illness had no place here. She would have plenty of time to consider death. Later.

Right now, she was going to focus on life.

She turned back toward the view, marveling anew. "I've never seen anything like this."

"Me, either," Padraig agreed. "Thank you, Mia."

Mia looked at him curiously. "Thank you?"

"For making that list. For dreaming big. For letting me tag along."

She laughed. "I'm letting you tag along? And here I was, thinking you were dragging *me* through that list. Helping me leave this life without regrets. I'm the one who should be saying thanks, Paddy. Everything about this trip has been a dream come true."

"Everything?" he asked, raising his eyebrows suggestively.

"Thought you outgrew all that horny stuff in high school."

He gave her an incredulous look. "Who said that? Jesus. Don't you know? Men get worse with age when it comes to sex, not better."

Mia rolled her eyes. "So noted. Come on. Let's go take a closer look at the cathedral."

After an hour or so of touring the grounds of Sacré-Coeur, Padraig suggested they find a café in Montmartre for lunch.

They held hands as they slowly meandered along the steep cobblestone streets of the town.

"What goes up, must come down," Padraig murmured on one particularly steep side street.

"I didn't realize we'd gone so far uphill. The funicular made it look quick and easy."

"What do you say we grab a table there?" Padraig pointed to a small café on the corner that had outdoor seating situated on the smaller side street. It looked private and quaint and perfect for a quiet, romantic lunch.

They claimed one of the tables and, after perusing the menu, they ordered a bottle of wine and escargot to start.

"Have you ever had escargot?" Padraig asked.

She shook her head. "No. Never. I just thought it sounded like something we should eat in France."

He laughed and handed her his cell phone. "You're gonna have to get a picture of me eating them or else Colm will never believe it. He constantly gives me shit for my meat-and-potatoes existence."

When the food arrived, they both made a face at the escargot served in shells.

"Well," Padraig said, picking up the tiny fork, "on the bright side, I'm pretty sure these things are swimming in butter."

He and Mia both stabbed one of the snails, taking a bite at the same time.

"Oh my God," Mia exclaimed, Padraig's face reflecting her response.

"Holy shit! That might be the best thing I've ever tasted."

Mia nodded, agreeing. "We need to order more."

He didn't even laugh. Padraig was already going back for another. "Is that garlic butter?"

"I think so."

The two of them polished off the plate of escargot—and an entire bottle of wine—with relish, then continued to explore Montmartre, shopping for souvenirs. Padraig found a bright yellow Tour de France flag to hang in the bar and some cool scarves for his mom and aunts.

They caught a cab back to the city center and found a nice restaurant for dinner near their apartment. By the time they returned home, Mia's feet were killing her.

"How far do you think we walked today?"

Padraig shrugged. "Miles, I suspect."

They kicked off their shoes near the front door and she limped over to the couch. Padraig started to follow her, then detoured to the kitchen, returning with two glasses of wine.

"Mother's milk," she joked, then sighed after taking a sip.

Padraig claimed the other end of the couch, lifting her bare feet to pull them over his lap. They drank in relative silence as both of them let the wine work out some of the kinks left behind after their busy day.

Because they were back in the apartment, and because Padraig's touches and kisses had kept her body

141

simmering with anticipation all day, her mind went straight to sex.

"So..." she started. "Last night was a bit of a surprise."

"What do you mean?"

Mia grinned. "You're such a teddy bear all day long, but put you in the bedroom and man...it's an entirely different story."

"I didn't hear you complaining last night."

"And you're not hearing me complain now. It's just you're so easygoing and sweet." She pointed toward the bedroom. "Where does that guy come from?"

"Define 'that guy'," he said, clearly enjoying her comments.

"Well, we're in Paris, so I actually have a pretty great comparison, even if it *is* Disney and way too G-rated for what we did last night. You go into full Beast mode, with that deep voice and the commands and total control."

"Did I scare you?"

She laughed, the sound full of incredulity. "Not even a little bit. God, it was a total turn-on. Maybe you noticed that part at the end where I thought my body was going to explode into a million pieces. The whole thing was just so..." She paused, trying desperately to find a word that would describe something that was ultimately indescribable. "So perfect."

"Mia."

"Yeah?"

"Put the wineglass down."

The tone had returned. And just like that, the weariness left behind after a day of playing tourist vanished. She set the wineglass on the coffee table, watching as he did the same. She felt a bit like the prey, waiting for the attacker to make his move.

Only she wasn't afraid.

Her feet were still on Padraig's lap and he used that to his advantage, gripping her ankles and using them to tug her until she was flat on her back on the couch. Then he parted her legs, coming down between them, caging her beneath him. His much larger size never seemed more apparent than these times, when she was buried beneath Mt. Padraig.

Padraig kissed her roughly. She could taste the passion, the desire. She'd never felt so adored or wanted. It was a heady thing.

Mia lifted her hands to his hair, but Padraig captured her wrists and pressed them to the cushion by her head.

"Leave them there."

She kept them where he placed them, even after he released her. Mia loved this feeling, reveled under his command. It felt good to let someone else take control. She was so freaking tired of constantly carrying every load alone.

Here with Padraig, she could trust him to give her what she needed without fear of being hurt—emotionally or physically. He cared about her, and she craved that attention more than she cared to admit, even to herself.

"God," she whispered when their lips parted briefly.

Padraig smiled at her reverent tone. "I can't get enough of you, Mia."

"I feel the same way."

"How would you feel about expanding on some of those X-rated *Beauty and the Beast* games?"

She giggled. "Be my guest."

He closed his eyes, shaking his head at her corny joke. "You're adorable. And mine."

"Yours." She wanted to say that, to try it on for size. She'd never given herself to anyone so completely.

Part of her wondered if it was because she was dying. It would stand to reason that her usual fears about commitment had faded away.

She rejected that idea instantly. This had nothing to do with dying. It had everything to do with loving Padraig. She loved him. Completely.

Mia was surprised when Padraig didn't continue the kiss. Instead, he sat up and looked around the room. She wondered what was going on inside his wicked mind when he gave her a grin that bordered on dangerous then stood up.

He walked over to the curtains. They were a chintz pattern covered with faded pink and blue flowers that looked like they'd been there at least thirty years. They were held open by two braided beige curtain ties that he slid free. Then he helped himself to a second set of ties as she watched.

Her heart beat faster as she nervously—and excitedly—waited to see what he would do next.

Padraig offered her a hand, helping her rise from the couch. "Let's go to the bedroom."

She followed him, her gaze dropping down to the ropes in his hand.

"Bondage," he said when they reached the room.

"What?"

Padraig pointed to the bed. "It's a four-poster. Haven't been able to get that fact out of my head all damn day."

"You want to tie me up?"

"Naked. Spread-eagle."

Her mouth fell open.

"But only if you want to," Padraig hastened to add.

"Wow."

He tossed the ropes onto a chair in the corner and stepped closer to her. "I didn't mean to scare you. It's too soon for that. I'm sorry."

She laughed. "You need to work on reading tone better. That wasn't a horrified 'wow'. Get the ropes."

Padraig studied her face, trying to decide if she was being honest. Her face was hot, a sure sign she was flushed.

"Hurry up," she prodded as she reached down to pull off her shirt. "Naked, you say?"

"Wow," Padraig echoed when her shirt and bra hit the floor.

She had no trouble interpreting *his* tone. Especially when she shrugged off her jeans and panties. Padraig hadn't moved a step as she undressed, his gaze traveling up and down and back up again.

His appreciative look gave her courage, made her feel like a seductress. Mia climbed onto the bed, lying on her back. Padraig didn't blink as she lifted her arms above her head, then opened her legs, displaying herself to him.

"Like this?" she asked, her voice husky with need.

The sound triggered the alpha male in Padraig. He walked to the chair to reclaim the ropes before returning to her. Kneeling on the mattress, he looped a braided cord around each of her wrists before tying them to the corner posts at the head of the bed. Then he repeated the action, securing her ankles to the footboard.

She tested the knots even though she had no intention of trying to break the bonds. Regardless, Padraig wasn't messing around. The ropes held tight.

He stood at the foot of the bed simply looking at her. She'd never felt more adored. If eyes could caress, his were stroking her into a frenzy.

Mia wiggled slightly, wishing he hadn't tied her legs so far apart. She needed some sort of stimulation, something to calm the storm brewing.

"Padraig," she whispered.

He was still fully dressed, that fact playing on her emotions, making her feel possessed. Owned. Only not in a bad way.

The beast had returned. And from the hungry look in his eyes, she could see he was ready to claim what was his.

"Don't talk, Mia. Or I'll gag you as well."

Her inner minx was somewhat tempted to force his hand on that. When Padraig reached into his suitcase and withdrew the single tie he'd packed, she thought perhaps he'd decided to do that anyway. Until the tie was placed over her eyes instead of her mouth.

A blindfold.

Mia wasn't aware of how much she relied on her vision until he took it away. She opened her mouth to speak, then recalled he'd taken that away as well. Not with an actual gag, but with his words, his command.

She closed her lips. Padraig obviously noticed, since he ran his finger along them and muttered, "Good girl."

Padraig continued to stroke her lips a few seconds longer before he pushed the tip of his index finger into her mouth. Mia closed her lips around it, sucking suggestively.

When he pulled it out, she waited, wishing she could see his face, see what was going to happen next.

She jerked slightly when she felt his wet finger on the tip of her nipple. It was a gentle touch at first, but soon he added his thumb and a pinch.

Mia's breathing hitched and it was on the tip of her tongue to ask him for more. Her pussy clenched, empty, needing.

Padraig's lips wrapped around the same nipple he'd been playing with, sucking deeper, harder.

Her hands instinctively moved, trying to grasp his head, to stroke his hair. It wasn't until that moment that the idea of being completely restrained truly sank in. She was helpless, vulnerable, dependent on him to provide the pleasure she desired.

She couldn't even speak, couldn't ask or beg. She really wanted to beg right now.

Padraig took his time, sucking on one breast, then the other, then back again. No one had ever paid so much attention to them. Ever. In fact, until Padraig, she hadn't realized exactly how much of an erogenous zone her breasts were.

"God," she whispered.

Padraig froze for a moment and his lips released her nipple with a soft pop. Though she couldn't see his face, she could just imagine his eyes narrowed in warning.

She bit her lower lip, not daring to even say she was sorry.

Padraig ran his fingers along one side of her face. "You're beautiful, Mia."

She started to smile—until he added, "But say one more word and I *will* gag you."

Mia pressed her lips together tightly to hold back her laugh. He probably didn't mean his words to be funny, and in truth, they weren't. She was simply overwhelmed by a sheer sense of giddiness.

It was as if someone had looked into her deepest, darkest, most secret fantasies and then created a man to match them.

Satisfied that she would remain quiet, Padraig returned to driving her insane by inches. No part of her was left untouched. He massaged her feet, her calves, licked the sensitive skin on the inside of her upper thighs, tormenting her when he refused to move closer to her center. He kissed her stomach and her neck as he held her bound, outstretched hands.

Worshipping.

If she could find one word to describe it, it would be that. Padraig was worshipping her.

It was beautiful. And yet she still wanted it to end.

Her nerve endings were on sensory overload. All of her was.

Her attempts to remain silent failed as she begged, cajoled, cried, then threatened. Padraig remained unmoved through it all, continuing with his sweet torture.

Finally, a million years later, he released her legs. She would have closed them, settling for even that minimum amount of relief, but he knelt between them, holding her open.

The blindfold was lifted next. She was ready to blast him, to curse him to hell and back for making her wait so long, but one look at his pained face told Mia he wasn't giving to her without some cost to himself.

She longed to touch him, but he didn't untie her hands.

"Please take off your clothes."

For the first time in nearly an hour, he granted her wish. He rose from the bed and started to undress. She tried to close her legs, but he gripped her ankle and shook his head.

"No."

It was one word, but it worked like magic when spoken in that deep, you-will-obey-me voice.

She forced herself not to move. Luckily, she was distracted by the shedding of his clothes. She would never tire of looking at him. He was broad-shouldered, muscular with an honest-to-God six-pack. She knew he liked to box. It showed in his chiseled physique.

Her gaze dropped the same time his pants did. Padraig was rock-hard, his cock thick and long. If they hadn't been together last night, she would have worried about the fit.

Apparently, Padraig had pushed his patience to the same limits as hers. When he returned to the bed, he lined his cock up and thrust to the hilt in a rough move that sent her into orbit. He didn't pause, didn't give her a chance to adjust. Instead, he just kept moving, thrusting, pounding.

Padraig lifted her legs, holding them up, the crooks of her knees resting on his shoulders. The position allowed him to go even deeper. Within seconds, she was there.

Mia cried out loudly as she came, but Padraig just kept moving. It was too much and not enough...all at the same time.

She couldn't get any air to her lungs and her heart thudded so loudly, she felt deaf to everything around her.

Still, Padraig pounded, took, claimed.

Her second orgasm came right on the heels of the first, helped along by Padraig's finger on her clit. He rubbed it firmly, stroking it with the same speed he was...fucking her. God. There was no other word for it.

Padraig was fucking her. And she never wanted it to end.

Mia was vaguely aware of the fact she would likely have a few bruises tomorrow. And maybe a hickey or three, she thought, as Padraig's lips descended on her neck, kissing, sucking and biting.

She thrashed, trying to break free from the ropes still binding her arms to the bed. She felt the need to leave a few marks of her own. Padraig grinned at her efforts, but made no move to release her.

"Mine," he growled.

He touched her clit once more, and this time he joined her, the two of them coming together loudly, a mass of heat and moisture. The room had been chilly when they'd first entered, but Mia suspected the temperature had risen to well above a hundred. At least in the bed. Or maybe just her body. She felt feverish, stunned.

Padraig dropped to the mattress next to her heavily, the bed rocking as if a boulder had just been tossed into a calm lake. They both lay on their backs, their breathing rapid and loud as they stared at the ceiling.

Mia feared Padraig had fallen asleep when, after several minutes, he didn't speak. He turned toward her eventually, reaching up to untie her.

"Did I hurt you?" he asked, concerned.

She nodded. "Oh yeah. Total Beast."

He pushed up to his elbow, upset and intent on examining the damage, when she started to laugh. It was more air than sound, her breathing still labored.

"Paddy." She put her hand on his chest to stop him. "Lay back."

He tilted his head, frowning. "Why?"

"Because I'm not going to be the only person to leave Paris with some lovely reminders of tonight."

She pushed lightly and he followed her lead, falling back to the bed. She leaned over and bit his tight brown nipple, showing him exactly what she meant as she made certain to leave an impression of her teeth.

He grunted.

"Oh, sorry. Did that hurt?"

Padraig placed his hand on the back of her head. "Yeah. Do it again."

"You sure?"

He laughed. "Be my guest, Beauty."

Chapter Eleven

May 12

Padraig walked out of the kitchen as Mia unlocked the door to her apartment and tossed down her workbag.

"Hey, stranger," she said tiredly.

They had been home nearly two weeks, and he was still struggling to get back into the daily routine.

"Rough day?" he asked.

She shook her head. "Nope. Just sucks to be back at work after the best vacation ever."

Padraig walked over and kissed her. "You can say that again. I was whipping up some dinner for us."

Since their return, Padraig had essentially moved in with Mia. Neither of them really discussed it. The decision was sort of made tacitly. They didn't want to spend even a single night apart, so he stayed with her. Each day, more and more of his personal things found their way over to her place. He had things hanging in the closet, tucked into a couple drawers in her dresser, and sitting on half the counter space in the bathroom.

Crazy thing was, it felt like he'd always lived here. There was no adjusting to cohabitation. One minute he was living in the Collins Dorm, the next he was with Mia. Both places felt like home.

"You don't have to work tonight?" she asked.

"Nope. It's my night off. Just going to be you and me, a pile of spaghetti and Netflix. Figure we can binge-watch something.

She smiled brightly. "Sounds like heaven."

Then she rubbed her temple.

"Do you have a headache? I can grab one of your pills."

"Oh, no." She lowered her hand, and it was obvious she didn't realize she'd been rubbing her brow. "Actually, I was thinking about that today. My headaches are getting better. I don't get the terrible ones as much as I had been, and even the dull, aching ones aren't as bad."

"That's good." Padraig was glad to know she wasn't in as much pain. She'd only gotten one more really bad headache after the one in Florida, and it hadn't been quite as brutal.

She reached for her bag, drawing out her laptop and setting it up on the dining room table. "Anyway. It got me thinking." She clicked on her keyboard, searching for something.

Padraig walked to stand behind her, looking over her shoulder. "About what?"

"Look what I found in one of the medical journals." She pointed to one line on the screen and started reading aloud. "These cancers are usually fatal, although prolonged survival does occur in a small minority of patients."

He nodded, struggling not to read on to the parts that said stuff like "surgery not possible" or "radiation only prolongs life for a few months" or "malignant."

"What are you saying, Mia?"

152

"I think the tumor is shrinking, all on its own. I don't think this thing is going to kill me."

Before Padraig could reply—God, what the fuck could he say to that?—she closed her laptop and walked to the kitchen with a definite spring in her step.

Mia thought she was getting better?

Padraig claimed the chair she'd just vacated, trying to wrap his head around what she'd just said. He was perfectly aware of the five stages of grief. His mother had given him a website link that described them, from the point of view of the dying person as well as the people close to that person. He'd looked it up one night before his trip with Mia, trying to find ways to understand what she might be going through.

Lately, he'd caught himself trying to figure out what stage he was in. As his feelings for her deepened, he had definitely stepped on that scale. While it appeared Mia was either stuck on or back to the first stage—denial—he had built a house on stage two—anger.

"Want me to dip this spaghetti out? It looks ready," Mia called from the kitchen.

He rose and walked to the entrance of the kitchen, leaning on the doorjamb. "Mia, I think maybe we should talk about that research."

She smiled. "I'm not sure there's much more to say about it. It just proves there's something Dr. Richards didn't tell me. Not everyone dies from this type of tumor. Some people live. I'm going to be one of those."

He sucked in a deep breath, his chest tight with the sudden onset of panic. "I hope that you are, but—"

Mia pulled the garlic bread from the oven, cutting him off. "This smells wonderful."

"Listen. I don't want you to get your hopes up about," he swallowed heavily, "that thing you read. I

153

think Dr. Richards probably has a better handle on your specific case."

Her smile faded, a scowl taking its place. "I'm sure every doctor says what I have is a death sentence, but there had to be some people who beat the odds, who outlived the stupid fucking timeframe. Otherwise that journal wouldn't have put that line in there."

He nodded, hating that he was dashing her hope, making her angry. Padraig couldn't decide if it was better for her mentally if he indulged her or if he helped her face the truth.

"Okay," he said at last. "Okay. You're right. Someone must have outlived the odds."

His agreement came too late. Mia's good mood was gone. "But you don't believe *I* will."

"I didn't say that."

"You think it. I can tell."

"I just want you to be prepared in case...things don't go the way you hope." Padraig's words came out slowly as he measured every single one.

"I'm not living on hope, Padraig. I can tell what's going on inside my head. The pain is less. That has to mean something."

He assumed it meant the pain medication Dr. Richards prescribed was working, but he didn't dare say that aloud. He was already walking a tightrope.

"You know, your next appointment is the day after tomorrow. Why don't we talk to Dr. Richards about your improvement? We can see if he'll do another scan. Confirm that the tumor really is shrinking."

"Fine. That's what we'll do. And then you'll have your proof." Disaster had been averted...sort of.

Mia was quiet as they ate, and after dinner, she said she was too tired for TV. Claimed she was still jetlagged and worn out from work and that she just wanted to turn in early.

He bid her goodnight, flipping mindlessly through the channels, playing their conversation over and over.

A quick glance at the clock told him it was only nine thirty. Business at the pub would be slowing down.

He stood up, grabbing his phone and keys, then jotted out a quick note that said, "Running down to pub for a little while. Back in a few," and left it on the table by the door in case she woke.

His dad glanced up as he walked in, giving him a worried look. "Everything okay? Mia feeling all right."

Padraig nodded as he claimed a stool at the bar. "Wouldn't be here if she wasn't." Glancing around the pub, his suspicions were confirmed. The place was emptying out.

"Want a pint?" Dad offered.

Padraig shook his head, his response ringing yet another alarm bell for his father.

"You and Mia have a fight?"

Padraig rubbed his forehead wearily. "Yeah. I think we did."

"You think?"

"She came home from work today in a great mood. Showed me something on the internet that she read as…" He didn't even know how to describe it. He saw it as some meaningless aside tacked at the end of a whole article of bad news. She read it and found hope.

Dad sighed. "She thinks she's going to get better."

"Yeah." Padraig had been through two doctors' appointments. He'd seen the CT scans, seen the tumor, heard about the precariousness of its location, how surgery wasn't possible, why chemotherapy and radiation would—at best—slow it down for a few months. That stupid line didn't change any of that.

"Sort of makes sense, don't you think?"

Padraig gave his dad a confused look. "I guess. I mean, obviously she doesn't want to die."

"Paddy. She's happy. She's in love. Given what you've told me about her past, it doesn't sound like she's had much experience with either of those things. You've given her a pretty strong reason to want to live, to have more time."

Padraig hadn't considered that. Guilt suffused him. "Shit."

His dad reached across the bar and patted his hand. "I didn't say that was a bad thing. Jesus, son. You built a friendship with that woman and rather than run away or deny your feelings for her, you embraced the relationship that evolved from that. It was a brave thing to do."

"I'm not brave, Dad. I'm fucking terrified. Every minute. I don't want to hurt her. And I don't want to lose her."

"The way I see it, there's only one of those things you can control."

Padraig hated that answer. Mainly because it was true.

Dad squeezed his hand. "So take control of that part. Give Mia what she needs from you, support her, calm her fears, give her a shoulder to cry on. I could tell when the two of you walked in here last week after that trip that you'd both turned a corner. You've committed to each other for the time you have left. Maybe you didn't make that decision consciously, but it was made just the same. You love her, right?"

"So much."

"Then let go of the shit you can't control and take charge of the rest—the love, the commitment, the relationship. Figure if you concentrate on that, it'll lessen some of your frustration over the rest."

Padraig smiled. He'd been right to come here. As always, his dad found the way to make him feel better.

With his father's advice to bolster him, Padraig felt ready to take on the world. "Okay. I will."

***

May 14

That resolve weakened two days later when he and Mia walked out of the doctor's office. The tumor wasn't shrinking, and Dr. Richards believed the headaches hadn't actually gotten better. It was simply that Mia's tolerance for pain had increased.

"He said the tumor hadn't grown," Padraig said when they climbed into the car. While Mia's hope had been dashed to pieces, Padraig had found some small comfort in the fact the tumor was the same size. "Not a bit in a month. Maybe that means his timeline is wrong. This thing isn't going to take over as quickly as we feared."

It was mid-May. The doctor had originally given her until September.

Padraig kept thinking about that birthday wish. It was just one more month. Surely the fucking tumor could wait one more goddamn month.

Mia didn't reply, didn't even look at him.

Padraig grasped for something, anything that might pull her out of the depression that was settling over her like a heavy, dark cloud.

"Want to go out for lunch? We could head down to the Inner Harbor, grab an outside table by the water."

"I'm not hungry. I just want to go home. And you have to go to work."

"I can call one of the other bartenders, Mia. Trade shifts so I—"

"No," she said loudly. "I don't want you to do that. I just need a little time by myself."

He wasn't sure if that was the best thing, but he couldn't exactly force her to accept his presence. Maybe a bit of time to digest the news would do the trick. She'd find a way to deal with this blow, the way she had all the others, and things would go back to normal.

Or at least as normal as they got when you were living with a bomb in your head and no wires to cut to kill the detonator.

"Okay," he said at last. "I'll just be at the pub. If you need anything, all you have to do is call and I can be home in five minutes."

She didn't reply until he pulled up in front of their apartment. "I'll be fine."

Mia got out of the car and walked inside without a wave or word of goodbye. It took everything Padraig had not to park the car, run up the stairs after her and hold her until the dark feelings went away.

Instead, he drove to the gym, pulled on a pair of boxing gloves and beat his anger out on the heavy bag until his arms and shoulders burned with pain and he couldn't lift them anymore.

***

May 17

Padraig came home from the bar. It was well after midnight, but he wasn't surprised to find Mia sitting in the dark on the couch.

She had taken up residence there right after the visit to see Dr. Richards, and she'd remained there for three days. No amount of cajoling from him, his mom, Kelli, Colm or Pop Pop could budge her.

Mia had gone to a very dark place in her head, and Padraig was starting to fear she'd never come back out again.

"You're up late," he said, trying to adopt a casual tone, trying to drag them back to something tolerable. Seeing her like this, quiet, numb, defeated, killed him. Every morning, he woke up and died a little more inside.

He wanted to rage, to scream at her, tell her to snap the fuck out of it, but he couldn't. Jesus. He wouldn't.

She was dying.

Padraig had put himself in her shoes countless times over the past two months, and every single time he found himself exactly where she was right now.

Broken. Hopeless. Alone.

He could stay with her 24/7, surround her constantly with his family and friends, and Mia was still going to be alone.

His physical presence, his love, his desire to hold on to her wouldn't change that. Mia was on a journey that he simply couldn't take with her. He might drive her to the train station, but that was it. He'd go back home, and she'd go...

Mia seemed to have run out of tears, but Padraig hadn't. He felt his eyes filling up. He used to pride himself on his strength, his ability to control pain.

Turned out he just hadn't felt true pain. Until now.

"Want to go to bed?" he asked, unable to hide the huskiness in his voice that betrayed his sadness.

She shook her head but didn't reply. The past few nights, Padraig had left her alone, let her sleep on the couch, thinking he was respecting her privacy.

He couldn't walk away from her again.

Dropping down to the couch next to her, he blew out a long breath. "How about a bedtime story?"

She looked at him—really looked at him—for the first time in days, and he latched onto that response as hope.

She didn't give him a yes or no, but he forged on anyway.

"My Pop Pop always used to tell me this one about St. Patrick. I was named after my grandfather, but he was named after the saint."

Padraig hadn't thought about the story in years.

"Once upon a time, there was a man named Patrick, and he lived in this magical place called Ireland."

The corners of Mia's lips tilted upwards at his dramatic fairy-tale voice. "I'm pretty sure Ireland is just a country. No magic."

Padraig pretended to be horrified. "I beg to differ. Ireland is the most magical place in the world—full of fairies and unicorns and leprechauns."

"I stand corrected. Sounds like a wonderful place. Maybe I should move there. I could use a little magic."

Padraig let her comment go without remarking on it. He had her attention for the first time in days. He wasn't going to let her go back into her depression without a fight.

"Well now, I wouldn't start packing my bags yet. There's still the issue of the snakes."

Mia shuddered. "Snakes?"

Padraig nodded. "Ireland was full of them. All the nasty varieties too. Not your peaceful little black snakes."

"No snake is peaceful."

"The king agreed with you. So much so that he declared whoever could get rid of the snakes could marry his daughter."

"The daughter was forced to marry the best exterminator? Lovely story."

Padraig snorted at her crinkled nose. "It wasn't as bad as that. After all, Patrick was a strapping, good-looking guy and he had the hots for Princess Maureen. She looked a lot like you. Red hair, bright green eyes."

"Brain tumor?"

Padraig narrowed his eyes, but before he could say anything, she sighed and muttered a soft, "I'm sorry. Tell me more."

"Patrick was getting pretty frustrated because, just like all the other guys in Ireland, he fancied Maureen, but he didn't know how to get rid of the snakes. But his luck changed one day when he caught a leprechaun named Seamus."

"He caught it?"

"Oh yeah. Leprechauns are wicked fast and hard to catch. If you manage to grab one, they have to take you to their gold."

"So Patrick got Seamus's gold?"

"Nope. He got something better. He got a magic flute."

Mia frowned. "I'm failing to see how that's better."

Padraig chuckled. "Patience, woman. Whenever Patrick started playing that magic flute, snakes would come out to listen."

"Oh yeah. That is definitely not better than gold."

Padraig ruffled her hair. "You're a hard person to impress. You're also failing to see. Patrick would play his flute and walk around town. All the snakes followed him, so he led them straight to the sea. Then he got on a boat, continued playing, and the snakes slithered right into the sea and drowned."

"No more snakes." Mia's eyes lit up. "And he got to marry the princess."

"Yep. He and Maureen lived happily ever after."

"Happily ever after," she repeated softly.

"I take my name very seriously, Mia."

She tilted her head, confused. "Okay."

He scooted closer to her, running his hand through her hair. "There are a lot of snakes squirming around inside you, scaring you, making you sad."

She sniffed, tears wetting her lashes. "I'm sorry I've been so—"

Mia didn't finish. He wouldn't let her. Instead, he kissed her softly.

"I'm going to drive those snakes out. I'm going to do everything in my power to make you happy. I swear it."

"You do make me happy, Paddy. I just…it's hard sometimes to keep feeling positive, optimistic." She wiped her eyes, then said, "You know, my name has a meaning too. It means 'wished for' or 'mine'. My grandma picked it out. Said I was her greatest wish granted."

"It is the perfect name. Mia. Mine."

Padraig kissed her again, making certain she didn't doubt that claim. She *was* his.

"Even if you drive the snakes away, Paddy, nothing will change."

"Everything has changed. For both of us. We're going to fill whatever time we have left with love and laughter and happiness. You still have the power to direct your course. To get the happily ever after you want. Don't lose sight of it. Reach for it. Grab it and hold on with both hands."

"Paddy," she whispered. "Can we go to bed?"

He helped her rise from the couch, leading the way as they walked to the bedroom. They moved slowly as they undressed each other, kissing and touching and caressing.

Then he laid her down on the bed, sliding into her slowly as she wrapped her arms and legs around him.

Padraig set a gentle pace, wanting her to feel how much he wanted her, needed her. Loved her.

They came together, crying out their release in unison. Then Padraig pulled her close as she cuddled next to him.

Several minutes later, he felt her shaking.

He lifted his head, concerned she was crying. Instead, he found her trying to hold in a laugh.

"Something funny?" he asked with a grin, pleased to see she'd turned a corner, found her way out of the darkness.

Mia's hand crept down his stomach until she could take his soft penis in her hand. "That's quite a magic flute you've got," she teased.

Padraig laughed as he tickled her. "Give me a few minutes to catch my breath and I'll play you another tune."

Chapter Twelve

June 28

Padraig grasped Mia's hand, leaving their luggage in the car.

She pulled back. "What about the bags?"

"Later," he said. "Aren't you excited? Why wait?"

She laughed and followed him through the hotel lobby to the door that led to the outdoor pool.

"This resort is incredible." Mia's eyes flew around, trying to take it all in. She'd never stayed in such a nice hotel. In addition to the outdoor pool, there was an indoor one, a tiki bar, outside seating at the restaurant and—she sucked in an excited breath—beyond those dunes, the ocean.

She and Padraig had fallen into a routine in the past month, waking up in each other's arms, showering, dressing, eating breakfast together before she went to work. On nights when he worked, she sat at the end of the bar and had her dinner, chatting with him as he poured drinks.

Last night, he'd surprised her by taking the night off to pack for this impromptu trip to Wrightsville Beach, North Carolina. Apparently, he'd found Shell Island Resort online and noticed they had a special weekend rate going for that very weekend. The next thing she knew, she was packed for the beach with just a moment's notice.

She loved Padraig's impulsiveness, his sense of adventure. For most of her life, she'd simply been stuck in a rut, a creature of habit, a slave to routine.

With Padraig, every day was different, fun, full of surprises. Sometimes he would stop by her work to surprise her with lunch. Twice, she'd woken up to find a rose on her pillow. More than a few times, he'd turned on music, grabbed her hand and danced her around the kitchen, slow or fast or silly, depending on his mood.

And now, another item was about to fall off her list of regrets. Padraig had already helped her tick off so many of them.

They'd gotten up at the crack of dawn, loaded his car with borrowed beach chairs, pool towels, and sunscreen. Padraig had found an oldies station on the radio, and they'd belted out "Freeze Frame", "Come Sail Away" and "Melt with You" at the top of their lungs. She'd grumbled a bit about the long drive, but with Padraig, she'd discovered the journey was just as much fun as the destination. So, eight hours later—after stops for gas, food, car treats, and a random stop at Bass Pro Shops—they'd arrived at the ocean.

She followed Padraig up the wooden steps, then stopped, gasping as she got her first glimpse of the ocean.

"Oh my God!"

Padraig grinned. "Come on." At the foot of the stairs, he kicked off his flip-flops and encouraged her to do the same. They left them there and walked barefoot in the hot sand toward the water's edge.

Mia struggled to take it all in, the roaring sound, the salty smell, the endless expanse of gray-blue water.

As they got closer to the Atlantic Ocean, Mia started to run, laughing, Padraig right beside her.

She pulled up just short of the white foam.

"Don't stop now. This is the best part." Padraig placed his hand on her waist, holding her close as they dipped their toes in. It was surprisingly cold.

Taking a few more steps, Mia felt the waves crashing over her legs, soaking the bottom of her shorts.

"Guess we should have put on our bathing suits first," Padraig said, when one strong wave splashed right up their backs as they turned away, trying to minimize the damage.

Mia laughed and shook her head. "There was no time."

Twisting back to the watery horizon, she threw her arms out to the sky, feeling free and at peace. "I had no idea it would be so massive. I mean, until you see it in person, you can't really understand the actual enormity of it. It's endless."

"Yeah. I always feel overwhelmed by it. And I've been to the beach a ton of times. It always puts life into perspective for me."

Mia considered that and nodded, feeling her own worldview knocked sideways a bit. "It makes me feel very, very small. Not in a bad way. Compared to the ocean, my life is the blink of an eye. One second in eternity."

"That's it exactly. The ocean has a way of humbling a person. And at the same time, I feel blessed to be here. To have this single second in eternity to make my mark."

Mia smiled. "You have a very romantic soul, Paddy."

Her words seemed to change something for him. His face was serious as he pulled her out of the water. They stopped just short of where the white foam ended.

"I was going to do this later, but now feels like the perfect time."

She tilted her head. "To do wha—?"

She stopped mid-word when Padraig dropped down to one knee in the sand.

"Paddy," she whispered, unable to hear her own voice over the thunder of the sea and the waves crashing inside her head.

"Mia Curtis. I know we haven't known each other a long time, but if I've learned anything these past few months, it's that it isn't the minutes that count. It's the way we fill that time. I've fallen so deeply in love with you, I can't even remember a moment when you weren't with me. I want to be with you, Mia, as your best friend, your lover and your husband. I want to spend every day from now until…whenever…with you."

He reached into his front pocket and pulled out a small box.

Mia wiped away the tear that got away from her, shaking her head slowly. "Please, Paddy. You can't—"

"Marry me, Mia."

"You know—" she started.

Once again, he interrupted her. "If there was no tumor, what would your answer be?"

"There *is* a tumor."

"Answer the question."

"I would marry you."

He smiled, but her heart cracked at the sight of it. She loved him just as deeply. Deeply enough that she would do whatever it took to protect him.

"Paddy. I said I *would* marry you. Not that I will."

He opened the box, and she gasped at the beautiful ring inside. Every dream she'd ever harbored as a young girl of finding her Prince Charming, the man who would love her no matter what, was coming true.

"It's beautiful."

He pulled the ring from the box. "It's yours."

Her hand was curled in a fist as she tried to find the strength to do the right thing. The problem was, marrying Padraig felt like the rightest thing in the world.

Mia bit her lower lip, struggling, wrestling with herself.

Padraig didn't push the issue. The gorgeous, patient man just waited, gave her time to come to the answer on her own.

"In October."

"What?"

"I'll marry you on my birthday. October second."

Padraig sighed, clearly not happy about the idea of waiting. But this thing between them was still too new. And she wanted to make sure Padraig understood completely what he was proposing.

"Mia," he whispered. "Please."

"It's three months, Padraig. Just three..." She couldn't finish the last. Jesus. Three months was basically all the time she had left if Dr. Richards was right.

He closed his eyes and she half-feared, half-hoped he'd take the ring back. Saying no would be the kindest thing. Getting married had been an item on her bucket list, one she had no expectation of fulfilling. However, over the past few months, marrying Padraig had moved into the number one position on the list. There was nothing she wanted more.

Padraig's eyelids lifted slowly, and she knew he wasn't taking the ring back. "Will you marry me on October second?"

Slowly, she unclenched her fist, holding her hand out to him.

Padraig's smile burst through, brighter than the sun. "Say yes, Tilly Mint. I need to hear it."

"Yes," she said, her voice breaking on her happy tears.

The wedding vows included for better or worse. God knew she and Padraig had already walked the razor's edge between those two things a few too many times.

He slid the ring on her finger then stood up to kiss her. She wrapped her arms around his neck, laughing when he lifted her and spun her around.

They kissed another minute more before a man stepped closer.

"Not going to lie, I was holding my breath there, afraid she was going to turn ye down, mate."

The stranger had an Irish brogue. Padraig grinned at the fella's joke, but it was obvious he didn't know the man, either.

"Oh, sorry. Name's Seamus. I'm just here on vacation. Was walking by when ye dropped down to one knee. Looked around and realized you two were alone, so…" He smiled at them sheepishly. "I recorded it."

He held out his phone and, sure enough, there was Padraig, holding out the ring.

"Thought you might like to have the moment documented. Had a few hairy moments there, thinking I might actually be recording your heartbreak. Glad it turned out well."

Mia giggled, delighted by the man's friendly, funny banter. The fact that his name was Seamus only made it all so much better. It was on the tip of her tongue to tell Seamus about Padraig's wand and the leprechaun with the magic flute.

"Gotta admit, you've got style, mate. Proposed to my gal one night in a pub, both of us pissed. She still gives me bloody hell for my lack of romance. So if ye want to give me your email address, I can send ye the video. Then I'm going to have to delete the damn thing. If my wife sees it, I'll never hear the end of it."

"How long have you been married?" Padraig asked.

"Three years. Love the gal. She's American. Met when she was studying abroad. If ye can't tell from this brogue, I'm originally from Kerry. Ireland."

"My grandfather is Irish," Padraig said.

Seamus's eyes widened. "Is that right? Well, small world."

Padraig gave Seamus his email and the video switched hands.

"Sorry to interrupt your moment. Blame my lack of romance. Hope the two of you have a very happy life together." Seamus nodded in farewell and continued down the beach.

"What a nice guy," Mia said.

Padraig tucked his cell phone back into his pocket. "Pop Pop is going to love that story. Suspect he'll show everyone he knows that video in the pub. Not because of the proposal but because of the Irishman who recorded it. Can hear him now." Padraig went into a pretty decent impersonation of his grandfather. "He was Irish, he was, the man who recorded it. Full of romance, we Irish are."

Mia laughed. "I'm not sure how he can say that. Seamus admitted to proposing to his girlfriend during a fight."

Padraig tilted his head, confused, until a light appeared to go on. "What? Oh, no. They weren't pissed as in mad. In Ireland, pissed means drunk."

"Well, that clears *that* up. I was wondering why the woman would say yes if they were arguing."

"Let's go grab our bags and change into our bathing suits. After that long drive, I'm ready for a dip in the pool and a drink from that tiki bar we walked past."

Mia and Padraig spent nearly two hours alternating between splashing in the pool and sunning themselves. Mia couldn't stop sneaking peeks at the engagement ring, trying to convince herself that it was really there, that Padraig had truly proposed.

"Hungry?" Padraig asked.

She nodded, so they threw some clothes on over their almost dry suits and grabbed an outside table at the resort restaurant, eating a huge pile of firecracker shrimp. Their table overlooked the ocean, which was sparkling with the last rays of sun.

A man started playing guitar and singing, and Mia decided right then and there was the most perfect moment of her life...again. She'd had countless perfect moments with Padraig.

The singer performed a great mix of cover songs mingled with originals. She was especially moved by a slower one with lines that spoke to her.

I will always be your ladder. Climb to safety.

Padraig had become her ladder, offering her an escape and a safe place beyond. The song seemed to have the same effect on Padraig, who reached across the table to hold her hand. Neither of them spoke, but the electricity between them was growing. Pretty soon they'd need one of those Danger, High Voltage signs.

"Paddy," she said softly. "Take me to bed."

He didn't need to be told twice. He paid the bill and they returned to the room.

Once inside, they hastily walked to the bedroom, shedding clothing along the way. By the time they reached the bed, they were both naked.

Padraig pushed her to the mattress before coming down on top of her. He kissed her long and deep, his tongue and hers touching, tasting. She tightened her fingers in his hair, tugging on the thick mass.

171

He ran one hand along her side, from breast to hip and back again. Then he cupped her breast, tweaking her nipple, before leaning down to suck it into his mouth.

She wrapped her thighs around his upper legs, trying to guide him closer, determined to have him inside her.

Padraig would never be the type of man to be controlled in the bedroom. He always had his own agenda and he made sure it played out. Not that she minded. The man was a master at making her come, giving her mind-blowing orgasms. And usually two or three a night. With past lovers, she was lucky to achieve one lackluster climax. Padraig wasn't selfish in the bedroom.

Not that that was surprising. She'd never met a more generous, compassionate man. Everything about him was just...perfect.

"Paddy," she urged when he continued to play with her breast. "Please."

He lifted his head and winked. Then he drifted lower, his hot breath hitting her clit a split second before his tongue did.

"Ohmigod," she mumbled. Her arousal tripled when he took her clit between his teeth, teasing the turgid bit of flesh. "Please," she repeated. "Oh, please."

Padraig never responded to her pleading. She'd learned that in Paris. If anything, her cries only encouraged him to drive her desires higher.

Her hands were still in his hair, and it wasn't until she heard him grunt once that it occurred to her she was probably hurting him. She loosened her grip, moving her hands to fist the sheets when he pushed three fingers inside her.

Mia thrust her hips toward the glorious invasion, trying to push him deeper. Padraig placed his hand on her stomach and with a firm grip, held her against the bed.

"You're killing me!" she yelled at him.

He grinned and shook his head. "No, I'm not. Now be a good girl and lay still."

"Yeah," she said sardonically. "That's gonna happen."

He raised one eyebrow that let her know she would obey him.

She decided to try a different tactic, tilting her head and adopting a sweet smile. "Paddy," she purred. "Please."

"You sure you want to take that route?"

Mia batted her eyelashes. "I need you inside me."

"At some point, you're going to have to learn some patience."

"Why?"

"Because some things are better when you wait."

"I don't wanna wait." She fought not to wince at the definite vein of whine in that comment. Not that it impacted Padraig. She realized it didn't matter what she said or how. He was going to do this his way.

She blew out an exasperated breath. "Fine. Do whatever. You're going to anyway." She threw her hands up against the mattress in the universal sign for surrender and didn't bother to hide her annoyance.

Padraig shook his head just once. "Wow. You did it that time."

Before she could ask what, he'd tugged her to a sitting position on the bed. A brief one while he shifted to the edge. Within ten beats of her heart, he had her facedown over his lap.

"What the hell—"

Padraig spanked her ass. Not hard. It certainly didn't hurt.

So it wasn't the pain that had her struggling to get up. It was the idea of what he was doing.

Padraig slapped her again, only this one had a slight bit of sting to it.

"What do you think—"

Another slap. And still Mia tried to get up.

After the fourth spank, Padraig ran his finger along her slit. Mia's legs parted slightly—almost of their own volition—so he could get to the good parts.

He didn't take her up on her offer. At least, not right away.

He gave her a fifth and sixth slap, and this time he didn't hold back.

"Ouch!" she cried out, the impact reminding her to fight back. Briefly.

Her desire to get away vanished the second he pushed two fingers inside her. She was somewhat shocked to realize how wet she was. How hot. How freaking close to coming.

Padraig thrust in and out half a dozen times and Mia went light-headed, her vision blurry as her climax erupted.

Her orgasm seemed to surprise Padraig as much as her. He kept his fingers moving, drawing out the pleasure. He didn't slip them out until the storm had passed.

Then with a gentle hand, he lifted her until she was cradled on his lap.

Mia rested her head in the crook of his shoulder, feeling boneless, replete. It took her several minutes to find her voice.

"You spanked me." There was no accusation in her tone. It was actually on the tip of her tongue to ask if he'd do it again.

"I did. Did you like it?"

She lifted her head and shot him an incredulous look. "What do you think?"

Padraig chuckled. "You don't hold anything back."

"What do you mean?"

"I never have to wonder if you're with me. Really with me, in bed. Some women are easily distracted, too busy thinking about how they look or what the sex means emotionally to really be in the moment, to enjoy what's happening. You're always with me. Telling me what you want. Showing me how it feels with your hands and your cute little cries. It's hot, Mia. *You're* hot."

His cock was rock-hard and pressed against her hip. While she'd found her release, he hadn't found his. And yet he was content to hold her like this.

Mia turned to face him fully, reaching down to grip his cock. He sucked in a deep breath when she placed the head of it at her opening.

Padraig gripped her hips, and she thought he might take control again. She was pleased when he simply kept his hands there, letting her guide this moment.

Mia sank down slowly, kissing him. She wasn't the only one making sexy noises as she continued taking him in deeper and deeper.

She held still once he was lodged to the hilt, but only for a second or two as she tried to catch her breath.

Then she lifted again, pounding down harder and faster the second time. And the third and the fourth.

Mia rode Padraig for all of a dozen strokes before his dominant nature came roaring to the forefront. He lifted her even as he continued to move inside her, twisting her to her back on the mattress. Kneeling over her, he added even more force to the coupling, taking her with a passion that was overwhelming. Amazing.

They came together in a rush of words and movement. Padraig jerking roughly as he swore he'd love her forever. Mia gasping and scratching his back as she promised she would always be his.

After several minutes, Padraig moved and helped her shift so that they could both climb beneath the sheets. He tugged her close, her head resting on his chest.

Then he sighed and shook his head. "Damn."

"What's wrong?"

"I was going to bring you up here and make love to you. We just got engaged at the ocean. I was hoping to expand on my romantic gesture."

She giggled. "You don't think what just happened was romantic?"

"I tossed you facedown over my lap and spanked that sexy ass of yours, then let you ride me before taking you like a man possessed. Jesus, woman. You push all my hot buttons. I swear to God I lose all control with you."

She lifted her head, her eyes narrowed. "I've yet to see you out of control, Paddy."

He chuckled. "That's not what I mean. I wanted to turn on soft music, lick every inch of that silky skin of yours and take you gently."

She didn't say that sounded a bit tame and maybe even boring after everything he'd just given her.

"I don't need roses and romance, Padraig. I just need you. However you want me."

Her words didn't seem to calm him. Instead, they appeared to inflame him anew as she felt his cock begin to thicken against her stomach.

"However I want?"

She laughed, not even pretending to regret that offer. "Yep."

"So, say I wanted to take you out on that balcony, bend you over at the waist and fuck you from behind while the waves crashed on the shore in front of us. That would be something you'd be up for?"

She sat up, climbing out of the bed. It was dark outside and they were on the far end of the resort. If they left the lights off inside the suite, she doubted anyone would know they were even outside.

"Where are you going?" he asked when she reached the doorway of the bedroom.

"To bend over."

She didn't need to say another word. Padraig reached the balcony half a step behind her. And when her third orgasm of the night struck, she felt very much like the crashing waves of the ocean.

Wild, untamed. Free.

Chapter Thirteen

July 24

"Mind if I join you?"

Mia looked up and forced a smile at Padraig's aunt Lauren. "Not at all."

Lauren slid into the opposite booth seat. "Padraig told me you've been having seizures this week."

Mia nodded tiredly. It was one of the reasons she was now sitting at a table instead of on a high stool at the bar. Padraig was terrified she'd start to have a seizure and fall before he could get to her.

Dr. Richards had warned her since the very first appointment that she may have seizures. However, several months had passed and she'd forgotten.

So had Padraig. Mia was fairly certain the first seizure had taken at least five years off the poor man's life. They were curled up on the couch, watching television when it struck. They'd originally planned to go to the movies, but she'd been suffering from a rather bad headache, so they'd opted for an On Demand movie and popcorn at home.

She didn't remember anything about the actual seizure, just what Padraig told her afterwards. Apparently, he had asked her if she wanted more soda and she hadn't responded. He said she had a sort of confused, faraway look in her eye, and then she'd slumped back just before the shaking started.

Padraig had rolled her to her side, making sure she didn't fall off the couch. Then he'd called 9-1-1. Everything she knew about the seizure she'd learned at the hospital, listening to Padraig describe it.

Dr. Richards had met them at the ER and explained that these would probably become more common. He told Padraig he'd done the right thing, and then gently reassured them she didn't have to come to the hospital after every seizure. Padraig left the emergency room armed with a list of instructions, while she'd walked out with a worse headache and a sinking feeling in her stomach that wouldn't go away.

Of course, insult was added to injury when Dr. Richards said she shouldn't drive anymore. As if she wasn't a big enough burden, she was now responsible for Padraig having to get up early after long nights, working at the pub to drive her to the office.

"Yeah, I have. Three of them. But none have been as bad as the first one was. It lasted nearly a minute. The others have been much shorter, not as violent, I guess you could say. Problem is they make me wicked tired afterwards and I can't drive anymore."

Lauren nodded as she listened. Mia knew Padraig's aunt was a psychologist. She glanced over at her sweet fiancé and found him sneaking a peek at them. When he caught her looking, he turned away quickly.

"Did Padraig send you over to talk to me?"

Lauren smiled. "Actually, no. I wanted to speak with you. I mean, Padraig's worried about you, but I don't think he's seen how much these seizures are bothering you. I get a sense that you're not telling him everything about your feelings."

"What do you mean?"

179

"He said you'd gone through a bit of a depression a couple of months ago, but since then, you've been just fine, happy even."

Mia was about a hundred miles away from *fine* at the moment, and *happy* was residing on another planet light-years from her present location. After their trip to the beach and his romantic proposal, she'd been on a super high, ridiculously happy. The seizures stole that from her. Made her feel vulnerable, weak. Terrified.

But she'd dumped enough of her baggage on Padraig, so she'd put on a happy face and pretended. It was getting harder to keep up the pretense.

"Yeah," Mia said, adopting that fake voice that seemed to fool Padraig. "I'm fine."

Lauren tilted her head, studying her face too closely for Mia's comfort. "I'm sure the seizures are taking a toll."

Mia nodded, but didn't say anything.

"It's not uncommon to feel sad or anxious after one as well."

Mia lifted one of her shoulders in a defeated shrug. "I don't think it's the seizures that are causing those moods."

Lauren had brought a glass of wine to the table with her. She lifted it and took a sip. "No. I don't think it is. You know, depression isn't all that unusual."

"I'm sure it's not. Most people with a death sentence hanging over their heads are bound to get depressed about it."

"I wasn't just talking about people who are dying. Everyone suffers from depression. What causes the feelings may differ, but the results are the same."

"I know." Mia appreciated Lauren's reassurances, but she'd gotten the you're-not-alone speech too many times lately. It didn't change the fact that she felt very, very lonely.

"You've met Oliver, right?"

Mia nodded, grateful, if somewhat confused, by Lauren's abrupt change of subject. "Yeah. A few times." She'd gotten a kick out of Padraig's youngest cousin. He was only twenty, which meant he was living for his next birthday so he could start drinking at the pub with his older cousins. He was energetic, with a great sense of humor and that larger-than-life personality that seemed to be part of the Collins family's genetic makeup.

"He's a piece of work, isn't he?" Lauren asked with a grin that showed just how much she adored her son.

"He's great."

"I call him my miracle."

"Miracle?"

Lauren looked down at her wineglass, toying with the stem. "I had four miscarriages before he came along."

Mia sucked in a breath. Four. "I didn't know that."

Lauren shrugged. "It was years ago, and I don't talk about it much. I always kind of dreamed that I'd have a big family. And I knew Chad and Sean would be wonderful fathers."

Mia knew Padraig would be a great dad too. The thought sent daggers through her heart, as she realized his future children wouldn't be hers.

"It's hard when you want something so badly, your whole body aches with it. And when you just can't get there, when you can't get what you want, it's devastating."

Mia nodded. She wanted to live. Wanted it with an intensity that was more painful than the headaches. "Yeah. Devastating."

"And then Oliver came along. He was so precious and wonderful. Everything I'd dreamed of and more. But..."

"But what?" Mia asked, when Lauren's voice faded away.

Lauren looked at her with sad eyes. "I assumed that since I was able to have Oliver, I'd be able to have more."

"That wasn't true?" Mia wasn't sure why she asked the question. She knew Oliver was Lauren's only biological child.

"I wanted the big family, remember? I had two more miscarriages after Oliver, before Sean said enough. I know he looks like this big mountain of a man, but in truth, he's a marshmallow inside, and seeing me crushed each time a pregnancy ended was more than he could take. He said Ollie was enough. Said there were a ton of kids who'd already been born who needed parents and we were going to help raise them. The next thing I know, Chad has us all signed up as foster parents."

"It sounds like it all worked out."

Lauren nodded. "It did. After a while. The thing is, I still lost all those babies. I spent years wondering what they would have looked like, who they would have grown up to be. It took a toll and I couldn't seem to drag myself out of my own misery. I was stuck down in this pit of despair, and the walls were smooth and slicked with grease. There weren't any handholds, so I just kept slipping back down every time I tried to climb out. I couldn't find a way to escape."

Mia understood misery. She'd been excelling at it lately. "That's exactly how it feels. What did you do?"

"I'm a psychologist. And I'm married to one. Ever hear that saying, 'Physician, heal thyself'?"

Mia nodded.

182

"It occurred to me as I sat in my office, listening to others talk about their pain, that I was becoming a hypocrite. I offered them all this advice that I wasn't willing to take myself."

"What kind of advice?"

"The usual things, like eating better and exercising. And the harder things. Challenging negative thoughts, doing something new, trying to have some fun. I know those things don't *seem* difficult, but when you've been wallowing in your own negativity and anger and sorrow for so long, it's a hard slog."

"Did that work?"

Lauren took another sip of wine. "I sort of refined it to make it easier for me. Whenever I felt the walls closing in on me, I took a deep breath, looked around, and tried to find three good things about where I was at that moment."

"And that works?"

"Yep. I'll give you an example. Chad, Sean and I went to a concert at Wolf Trap last week. We got stuck in nasty traffic, showed up way later than I'd planned and we couldn't find a spot for our picnic dinner on the lawn. Wound up way in the back on a hill where we couldn't even see the stage. On top of that, I spilled the first glass of wine Chad poured for me on my pants. I'm wet and grumpy and ready to go home. Sean and Chad are completely oblivious to how pissed off I'm getting, which didn't help. I opened my mouth to suggest that we just pack it in."

"But you didn't?"

Lauren shook her head. "No. I caught myself. I took a deep breath, looked around and decided I was actually in a great place. It was a beautiful summer day, cool breeze and shade. We had yummy subs and wine and a soft blanket to sit on. The people around us were really nice and fun. When the music started, we stood up and danced our asses off. It turned out to be a fantastic night. One that I almost ruined with my foul mood."

Mia had been sitting in that booth for the past hour, stewing over everything that was wrong. Angry at the world. "Three good things?" Mia looked around the pub and realized that she could pick out three great things without even trying. Padraig was talking sports with Colm, the two of them in some serious discussion. There were several patrons laughing loudly as they relaxed with drinks after work, and Riley was telling a story to a table of diners in the restaurant that seemed to have them all on the edge of their seats.

Three things that made her happy. Padraig, his family, and this pub.

"Already got three, don't you?"

Mia smiled. "I do."

"Are you cheating and counting Paddy as all three?"

Laughing, Mia shook her head. "No. Although…"

Lauren rolled her eyes good-naturedly. "Oh, to be young and in love."

Mia didn't think Lauren was knocked out on either of those accounts. There was no denying she was still head over heels in love with her two husbands, and it wasn't like Lauren was headed to a nursing home anytime soon.

"I hope you don't think I'm trying to minimize what you're going through, comparing it to a silly concert."

"Oh no. I get it. I really do. I like the idea of being normal. God, if I thought about this tumor 24/7, I would have already gone mad, lost my mind completely. My best days are the ones where I go hours without remembering that I'm dying. Ordinarily, it's always there, always hovering in the back of my mind, sneaking in and sucker punching me. I love it when I can play a game with Paddy and his cousins upstairs or watch an entire movie or even spend an afternoon, working on a boring-as-shit spreadsheet at work and not remember. Not even once."

"Focusing on the good things helped me out of a dark place. I hope it will do the same for you."

"There would probably be a lot fewer depressed people in the world if everyone could manage to do that. Find the positives, seek out what makes them happy."

"Yeah. But then I'd be out of a job."

Mia laughed and gave Lauren a horrified look. "Well, we couldn't have that."

"You and Padraig are very similar souls."

Mia was taken aback by Lauren's observation. She had actually chalked their relationship up to one of those opposites-attract things. He was loud and boisterous and playful. She was quiet and serious and silliness didn't come natural. "How so?"

"You're both very kind and honest. And neither one of you is afraid to feel things deeply. If you were, you wouldn't have opened yourselves up to love at such a difficult, scary time. I think that's really brave."

"Paddy is the brave one. I'm the lucky one. I found him at a time when... I can't imagine doing this without him."

Lauren shook her head, her smile wry. "Lucky, huh?" Lauren reached out and took her hand. "You're one of the bravest women I've ever met, Mia. Never doubt that."

"Hey, Mia."

Mia looked up as Padraig called out her name. He was no longer beside the bar, but standing near the front door of the pub.

"Come here," he beckoned. "I have a surprise for you."

Lauren rose as well, following her. From her curious expression, it was clear Padraig's aunt didn't have a clue what was going on, either.

As soon as Mia reached the front door, Finn walked in with a squirming puppy in his arms.

"Take this beast," Finn said, handing the small dog to Padraig. "Little devil just chewed a hole in the passenger seat of my car!"

"I sent you with a crate," Padraig said, laughing as the dog tried to climb his chest to lick his face.

"Yeah. Good luck getting that tornado into a crate." Finn handed Mia a leash. "Or on a leash. I swear to God he's freaking Houdini. Managed to get that leash off three times. I have no idea how."

Mia hadn't stopped looking at the wiggly dog. "You got a dog?"

"*We* got a dog," Padraig corrected her. "And while I wasn't trying, it looks like I managed to find a badly behaved one, per your list."

Mia laughed as she reached out to stroke the dog's head. The second she touched him, he twisted in an attempt to get out of Padraig's arms and into hers. Padraig tried to hold him back, but Mia was already grabbing for him.

"He's hard as hell to hold onto, Mia," Padraig warned.

"I'll hold tight," she promised.

The puppy treated her to the same all-over face licking Padraig had received, but Mia didn't care. The tiny dog was the sweetest thing she'd ever seen. All her life she'd wanted a dog, but her mother had refused when she was a child, and after that, she'd never managed to find an affordable apartment that allowed dogs in Chicago.

"I love him," she said.

Padraig winked at her. "Damn. I had to wine and dine you and fly you to Paris to get those three little words. Wish I'd known licking your face would evoke the same response. Lot cheaper and quicker."

"What's his name? Where did you get him?"

"His name is up to you. A litter of pups got dropped off at the SPCA a couple of weeks ago. He's the last of the group."

"You are perfect," Mia said to the puppy, immediately going to baby talk though she didn't have a clue why. "Yes, you are! You are the most perfect puppy in the whole world."

"Thanks for picking him up, Finn."

"You might revoke that thanks after a few hours. I swear to God someone's been feeding him nothing but speed."

"I'll pay to get the seat patched up," Padraig offered, but his cousin just waved him off.

"My car is a piece of shit and you know it." Finn grabbed a seat at the bar and ordered a beer.

"Joel is here to finish up tonight's shift," Padraig said. "Thought you and I could take off early and introduce the pup to his new home."

"We don't have food or a bed or—"

"I bought it all yesterday and hid it in the trunk of my car. We've got everything we need." Padraig managed to get the leash on the dog, but he carried him most of the way back to the apartment, Finn's words about his leash-breaking skills resonating.

"Don't fancy chasing a puppy all over Baltimore," he said.

When they arrived at her apartment, Padraig put him down tentatively near a tree. Mercifully, the dog took him up on the invitation, marking the territory instantly.

"Fingers crossed that buys us a few hours without an accident." Padraig picked the puppy up and carried him upstairs to her apartment, not unfastening the leash or letting him down until he was safe behind closed doors.

She and Padraig laughed as the tiny dog ran around the apartment, taking in everything and nothing in his mad dash to race to the next spot.

Padraig reached out and pulled her toward him, giving her a quick kiss. "Nice to see that smile back on your face. I've been worried about you this week."

So much for hiding her sadness. She sucked when it came to fooling him.

"I'm better now. Talking to Lauren helped."

He tugged her into a warm embrace. "You could talk to me too if you want."

She pressed her face against his chest, soaking up the sweet smell of him, bourbon and soap. "I didn't want to keep dumping all my sadness on you."

Padraig kissed the top of her head. "I don't want you hiding anything from me, Mia. Definitely not the bad stuff."

"I know. I won't anymore. Promise. Besides, Lauren gave me a great coping strategy that I'm going to try. Sort of handy how you have a shrink in the family."

Padraig laughed. "One of the benefits of a huge family. You need a paper edited, a song written, a house built, your head examined, or a good meal and a stiff drink, we got you covered."

The puppy, finished with his explorations, had returned to them. He was jumping up and down in an attempt to get one of them to pick him up.

Padraig took the bait—and the wet kisses. "So, what are we going to name this little fella?"

"How about Seamus? That name seems to keep creeping up in our lives, whether it's leprechauns, wands or cheeky Irishmen."

Padraig considered and nodded. "I like it. A lot, and I think it suits the guy."

She and Padraig set up Seamus's food and water dish in the kitchen, played fetch with a soft toy in the living room, then debated where in their bedroom to put the dog's bed. That discussion was declared pointless when Seamus whined and tried to hop up on their bed. Mia lifted him up and the tiny puppy happily settled down at the foot of it.

"Are we letting him sleep in the bed with us?" Padraig asked, clearly not a fan of the idea.

For Mia, it wasn't even a question. "Of course we are. Look how sweet he is when he's asleep. Besides, I can cuddle with him on nights when you work late."

"Four months into this relationship and I've already been replaced by a dog."

Mia tugged off her clothes, pulling on the T-shirt she usually slept in when Padraig didn't immediately take it back off her.

He opted for sleeping in the nude, which suited her just fine. They climbed into bed, both laughing when Seamus crawled right up between them and settled back to sleep.

Padraig looked at her over the softly snoring dog's head. "I'm going to research obedience schools in the morning."

She giggled. "Don't know if it will help. Something tells me we're both firmly standing in the 'indulgent pushovers' camp."

Padraig didn't bother to disagree. It was obvious he knew she was right.

They lay facing each other, petting the puppy.

"I'm glad talking to Lauren helped," Padraig said after a few minutes.

Mia decided to take advantage of the opening he provided, bringing up a subject that had actually caused some of her darker moments this week.

"When I'm gone—"

"Mia," Padraig interrupted her immediately. He never let her talk about her coming death. Never let her say the words or admit that it was happening.

"Paddy. Please. I want to talk about this."

He closed his eyes and then, because he was wonderful and giving, he sighed and nodded. "Okay."

"When I'm gone," she repeated, "I think maybe you should consider talking to Lauren—or Chad, if you're more comfortable with him—about...stuff."

"Mia, I don't really want to think about life without you."

She gave him a smile. "And I think that's really sweet. But also really stupid."

He chuckled at her joke. Neither of them wanted to have this conversation, but Mia had things she needed to say, things that had been bothering her. Humor would make it easier.

She dove back in. "I'm not going to be here next year."

"Fuck. Stop. Stop it right now, Mia. I can't—"

She forged on. "I don't want you to be sad."

He rolled his eyes. "Now who's being stupid? Jesus. I'll be devastated."

Lauren had used that same word. There were so many people in so many different situations, and yet they all felt the same unbearable, heartbreaking pain. For the first time, Mia really didn't feel alone.

"Fine. Good. Be devastated. For a little while. Then stop being sad. You're only thirty-one years old. You have another fifty-plus years to think about. I want..." She swallowed. "I want them to be happy for you. We've spent so much of the past few months, living out *my* dreams. You've never told me what *yours* are."

"You," he said, without a second's hesitation. "You're my dream come true."

She let those words sink in deep, warming her straight to the core. "You're mine too," she admitted.

He placed his hand on top of hers, where she was still petting Seamus, and gave it a quick squeeze.

"I had a list of dreams," she said, not willing to let him off the hook. "Tell me more. Tell me the ones you're going to chase after..." She didn't add anything to the after. It always upset him, made him wince.

"I...I'm not sure anymore."

And with those words, he confirmed her fears. He was losing sight of his own hopes and dreams. She didn't want his future to end when she did.

"Tell me the ones that were there before me. Start with something simple."

"I want to go to the Super Bowl. And game seven of the Stanley Cup final, but only if the Caps are playing. And the World—"

She giggled. "Are there any goals that don't involve sports?"

"I always liked the sound of a cruise to Mexico."

"Oh!" Her eyes widened. "Dammit. I wish I'd thought to put that on my list."

He didn't tell her there was time because they both knew there wasn't. With the onset of the seizures, neither of them was comfortable with the idea of straying too far from her doctor.

"What else?"

"I'd like to take one of those charter boats out on the ocean and fish for tuna and bluefish, ride a donkey into the Grand Canyon, run a marathon, and hike a bit of the Appalachian Trail."

"Your list is longer than mine."

He was grinning. At least until her next question.

"Do you want to have kids?"

He froze, his refusal to respond to the question all the answer she needed.

"Of course you do. You're going to be an amazing dad. So, you'll fall in love again, get married and have a family."

He shook his head, but she didn't let him voice his refusal.

"You're too amazing, Paddy. Too full of life to not go out there and find love again. And you *have* to have kids. Maybe twin boys like you and your brother."

"God, no. Me and Colm were total pains in the ass. Not sure how my folks survived our childhood." He paused, then said, "I'd really like a little girl."

She imagined Padraig with a daughter on his lap. She could envision the girl in bib overalls with braids, giggling as her daddy tickled her. "I hope you get your daughter."

"I wish she could be yours too."

Mia swallowed deeply, determined not to cry. It was definitely time to return to humor. "What? Why would I want a kid when I have this adorable puppy hogging the bed?"

Padraig's smile was faint, but there.

"Go get your dreams, Paddy. Live every second of that life you've just imagined. Make sure you find the same happiness that you've given me."

He reached over and ran the back of his hand along her cheek. "Okay, Mia. I will."

"Good. Because I'd really hate to have to come back and haunt you."

He chuckled, then carefully climbed over the dog to cage her beneath him. He gave her a kiss that he clearly intended to take a lot further.

Unfortunately, his sudden movement woke Seamus, who thought it was playtime as he jumped on Padraig's back, then initiated a game of tug-of-war with the sheets.

They wrestled with the dog, and when they all three finally fell asleep again, Seamus was back in his place between them.

The new lord and master of the house.

Chapter Fourteen

August 19

"Pretty sure you're making Uncle Sean's life right now with this damn karaoke wish of yours."

Mia looked toward the stage, where Sean was setting up equipment with his husband, Chad. "Really?"

Padraig nodded. "Pat's Pub used to have a standard karaoke night—Sean's idea. Apparently, it was fun for about five minutes, then about three months into it, my dad put his foot down and said he wasn't going to spend every Wednesday night of his life, listening to a bunch of drunks butcher Michael Jackson, Mariah Carey and Prince. It was a brief run, and I think Sean was the only one who missed it."

"I can't wait to hear it."

Padraig gave her a funny look. "Hear it? Oh, hell no, sweetheart. You're singing it."

Mia bit her lower lip. "I know I said that I wanted to do that, but—"

Padraig cut her off. "You're not backing out."

"I'm not exactly the type of person who stands up in front of people and sings. And I'm not sure it's smart to drink the amount of alcohol required to give me that courage. I have enough headaches without adding a self-induced one."

"We'll do a duet."

She had seriously thought there was nothing Padraig could say that would convince her to get on that stage, but remarkably enough, that changed her mind in an instant. "That would be fun. What should we sing? Does Sean have a list of song choices?"

"Don't need it. We're singing the greatest love song in the history of music."

Mia wasn't sure she wanted to know what Padraig thought that was. He already had thrown very questionable "greatests" at her in the past, proclaiming *Jaws* the greatest movie—um, hell no—declaring *River Monsters* the greatest television show—in what world?—and insisting "I Don't Want to Miss a Thing" was the greatest rock ballad ever—as if Heart's "Alone" didn't even exist.

"Ooookay," she drawled slowly. "What would that be?"

He winked at her and simply said, "You'll see. I'll sign us up."

Mia took a sip of her beer as she shook her head. Pop Pop was sitting in his usual spot farther down the bar. He lifted his pint glass toward her in a silent cheers just before his oldest friend, Moose, sat down next to him.

"You all starting this confounded stuff up again. Noise pollution," Moose grumbled.

Mia giggled.

"What's so funny?" Kelli asked as she claimed the stool next to her that Padraig had just vacated.

"I think everything."

Kelli didn't even blink. "In this place? Yeah, that's pretty much always true. Whole family is bat shit and funny as fuck."

Mia tapped her glass against Kelli's. "I still can't believe you teach kindergarteners."

"Who do you think is responsible for my gutter mouth and alcoholism? Five-year-olds are vicious fuckers. People tend to let the adorable packaging fool them."

Mia had been around Kelli enough to know that she loved her job and her students quite dearly. And Padraig had set Kelli straight on multiple occasions, insisting her foul mouth and love of alcohol had always been there well before the job.

Padraig was glancing at Sean's music list over by the stage. She could tell by his grin he'd found the song he'd been seeking. He started to fill out one of the tiny pieces of paper.

"Padraig going to sing?" Kelli asked, noticing where Mia's attention lay.

"Yeah. Apparently, we're doing a duet. He won't tell me what song."

Kelli snorted. "Twenty bucks says it's 'Endless Love'."

Mia groaned. "Oh my God. Seriously? This is worse than I thought. He thinks *that's* the greatest love song in history?"

"Hell yeah. Probably not because of the words, but because of the singer. Padraig swears he sounds just like Lionel Ritchie."

"Better that than Diana, I guess."

Kelli choked on her beer as she started laughing. "We used to play this game in ninth grade where we'd play some of Paddy's parents' old music to see who could come closest to imitating the singer. We were all chorus geeks in those days, me, Colm and Padraig."

"All three of you were in choir in school?"

Kelli nodded. "Yep. Even had parts in the school musicals even though none of us was talented enough for a lead. One year, Colm had a nasty head cold during auditions and didn't even get a part. So he took over as stage manager, which he ended up liking more than being in the play. Fed into his massive control-freak nature."

Mia always enjoyed listening to Kelli talk about the past. She was a walking, talking encyclopedia when it came to Padraig's childhood, and Mia loved it. It wasn't that Padraig didn't share. It was just fun to get someone else's perspective on it all. Kelli never skimped on details and she never seemed to forget anything.

"Hey, would you want to do lunch tomorrow?" Mia asked. "I know school starts back next week."

"Sure. Just you and me? Girl date?"

Mia smiled. "Yeah. That's the plan. Thought maybe we could swap old stories. I like hearing about Paddy." She hoped to share a few of her own stories with Kelli. She knew that Padraig would lean on Kelli heavily after she was gone. Mia sort of liked the idea of giving Kelli some of her history. It wasn't the same thing, but it would be nice to think there was someone holding on to a few little pieces of her past for her.

"That would be awesome. I know this Mexican place that makes killer margaritas. But if we're swapping stories, you better come ready to do some talking too. I want to hear about your wild high school days, your sex regrets, and any other sordid stuff you've got. Need me to make a list so you can prepare?"

Mia picked up her phone and pretended to type a note. "Hang on a second. One-night stands, drunken brawls, what else?"

They laughed together even as Kelli said, "I'm totally not joking."

Wild Devotion

"I know," Mia said, as she glanced back at Padraig. He'd gotten shanghaied into helping Sean and Chad set up the sound system.

"You're going to take care of him, right?" Mia asked, the question popping out before she could think about it.

Kelli turned to face her. "Yeah. I've always had his back. I always will."

"Don't let him be sad for too long. You're good at making him laugh."

Kelli rubbed her forehead. "I fucking hate this conversation."

Mia reached out and grasped her hand. "Promise me?"

Kelli held on to her hand. "I promise, Mia. But…just don't be in a hurry to go anywhere, okay? I've already started working on the wedding ceremony and I've paid for the officiant's license. The entire thing is going to be stellar. I need you to live a whole lot longer."

Kelli had been thrilled when Padraig and Mia had returned from the beach with her wearing his engagement ring.

Originally, Mia had demanded that they wait for her birthday because she thought it was her way of protecting Padraig. However, the more time that passed, the more she realized that date was giving her something to live for. For weeks, she'd been immersed in wedding plans with Padraig's family. None of them seemed to question for a minute that the event wouldn't truly happen. Or if they did, they were doing a damn fine job of hiding those doubts from her.

She, Yvonne and Sunnie had gone dress shopping twice, Riley had at least three different running lists as the two of them planned the food for the reception, and Pop Pop had quickly requested the right to walk her down the aisle—she cried when he asked, so thrilled and touched that he wanted to.

Kelli patted her hand as she released it. And then quickly, smoothly, she took a heavy moment back to light. Padraig would definitely be in good hands when she was gone.

"So, how's your Diana?"

Mia winced. "Poor. Probably nonexistent. Don't suppose she was one of the voices you perfected back in high school?"

Kelli crinkled her nose. "Hell no. You're singing the damn love song with him. Besides, I've got my own shtick."

"Do I want to know?"

"I sing Joni Mitchell better than Joni Mitchell. Which reminds me, I need to go sign up. Don't want too many people to get in ahead of me because if this goes south and my ears start bleeding, I want to be able to skip out fast."

Kelli and Padraig said a few words as they passed each other.

"All set up?" Mia asked, sort of hoping the system didn't work.

"Yep. We're third."

Mia took a long chug of her beer, deciding to hell with it. She'd just suffer the damn hangover.

Padraig laughed at her. "Chicken shit," he teased.

She picked up a peanut from the bowl in front of her and lobbed it at his head. He dodged it. "Who's going first?"

"Sean insisted on an encore performance. Apparently, the last time they did karaoke, Ewan managed to get Natalie on stage to sing."

Mia was surprised to hear that. "Natalie doesn't strike me as the karaoke type."

"You're not kidding. And according to Sean, she's the world's worst singer."

That fact was proven when Padraig's aunt took to the stage to sing an old Wilson Phillips song. Mia bit her lip hard in an attempt not to laugh, even though Ewan was standing near the stage, cracking up. Mia realized Natalie was perfectly aware of her lacking ability, and not too bothered by it, when she flipped her husband the middle finger and kept going, her smile growing bigger by the minute as she swayed in time with the music.

Kelli came back over. "I changed my mind. Wild horses couldn't drag me out of here. This shit is epic."

Sean overheard her and made certain Tris, who was tending bar, had too. "Hear that, bro? Epic. I think it's time to bring back karaoke night."

Tris didn't even look up from the drink he was mixing. "Never gonna happen."

The next act, a regular at the pub, proved exactly why Tris had put his foot down all those years ago. The man had chosen to sing the oddest version of "America the Beautiful" Mia had ever heard in her life. It had actually taken her a minute to figure out what he was singing.

Moose shook his head and ordered another beer. "Noise pollution," he repeated.

Then, too soon for her comfort, Sean announced that it was time for her duet with Padraig. And as Kelli had predicted, it was "Endless Love." While Sean scrolled through to find the words on the screen, Kelli yelled out that Mia owed her twenty dollars.

Mia rolled her eyes, but she was too self-conscious and nervous to joke back. She hadn't realized how many people were in the pub until she'd stepped up onto the stage.

"Mia," Padraig said as he handed her a mic. "Just look at me. This is all in fun. No one's expecting to hear Teagan- or Sky- or Hunter-level talent. Besides," he leaned closer, "Sean put us in a great spot. There's no way we're going to suck as bad as Aunt Nat and the Lee Greenwood wannabe.

"Did Natalie throw her performance on purpose?" Mia asked, realizing Padraig had a point. Mia wasn't a great singer, but she was capable of carrying a tune.

"God, no. I wish. That's actually her real singing voice. She's called me every single year of my life to sing 'Happy Birthday' over the phone. It's brutal. Hilarious. But brutal."

"Are you two ready?" Sean asked.

Padraig gave her a quick kiss on the cheek, then turned and nodded to his uncle.

The first few strands of the piano played, and then Padraig took her hand, cheesing it up big time as he performed a seriously great Lionel Ritchie impersonation.

She joined in just a beat behind where she was supposed, but soon caught up. Padraig had the song memorized and never once looked at the monitor. If she'd been home alone, she suspected she would have known the whole thing by heart too. However, nerves had jarred all the words loose, so she had to keep glancing at the screen for help.

By the end of the first chorus, though, her anxieties had melted away. Probably because Padraig was making her laugh with his over-the-top, eyes-closed-as-if-in-pain, Stevie-Wonder style head swaying. Everyone was laughing, Mia included, and somewhere in the midst of it all, he managed to convince her that "Endless Love" was indeed the greatest love song in history.

They received the first standing ovation of the night when the song ended, and then, to everyone's delight, he dipped her in a very dramatic, old-fashioned kiss that would have made Rhett Butler proud.

The two of them returned to the bar, wetting their whistles as another regular took a turn, belting out a great version of John Denver's "For Baby."

"Glad we didn't have to follow her," Mia said, seriously impressed with the woman's voice.

"Told you. Sean set us up perfectly."

They spent another hour at the bar, chatting with family and friends and enjoying the karaoke. Kelli hadn't exaggerated her Joni Mitchell chops. She belted out a version of "Big Yellow Taxi" that brought the house down.

Mia told her how amazing she was after it ended, while Padraig simply ruffled her hair and called her a "show-off."

After a couple of really bad renditions of Michael Jackson, Padraig said, "I don't think it's going to get much better at this point. Want to go home?"

She nodded as they said their goodbyes, then walked to her apartment hand in hand.

"Good night?"

"Oh yeah. I'm glad you encouraged me to sing. It was fun."

"Everything is fun with you, Mia."

She grinned. "I'm pretty sure you're the only person to ever think that."

He wrapped his arm around her shoulders and kissed the side of her head. "I'm pretty sure I'm not. My family loves you. And there's not a doubt in my mind Kelli prefers you to me."

"We're going out to lunch together tomorrow."

"She told me. Don't let her talk you into more than two of the margaritas. I know that Mexican place where

Mari Carr

she's taking you, and they are potent. Two of those and you'll be singing without the karaoke machine."

She nuzzled closer to him. "So noted."

Seamus was more than ready for them when they returned, so Padraig put on his leash and they walked back downstairs and around the block with him a couple of times.

While both of them were starting to wind down, the same couldn't be said of Seamus, who was bouncing happily between them. Padraig joked they would have been better off naming him Yoyo, because that was what he looked like whenever they put the leash on him.

Once they were back in the apartment, Padraig turned on some music, searching until he found what he was looking for.

"More Lionel Ritchie?" she asked.

He pulled her into his arms for a slow dance, softly singing "Truly" along with Lionel. They swayed together as Seamus circled their feet.

Mia loved the feeling of his cheek pressed against hers, the way his beard tickled. His hands stroked her back as they moved. Every now and then, one would drift lower to cup her ass. She ran her fingers through his thick hair. When the song ended, he touched his forehead to hers.

"I love you, Mia."

She lifted her face, initiating the soft kiss. It would have lasted longer, would have turned into something much more, if Seamus hadn't jumped up against Padraig's legs and started barking.

"Someone is getting jealous," he joked.

Mia bent down to pick up the squirming puppy. "Aw, baby. Are you feeling neglected?" Seamus licked her face, then twisted his head and added some to Padraig's cheeks and chin.

203

"I love our little family," Padraig said as he turned toward the bedroom. "Let's get that boy to bed."

It took Mia a second or two to move as his words washed through her.

Family.

Padraig had given her the perfect family, offering not only himself, but his own large, crazy, boisterous Collins clan and Seamus.

She had a family.

Chapter Fifteen

September 20

Padraig dragged himself into the bedroom well after midnight. He was looking forward to falling face down on the soft pillow and catching some serious zzz's. Mia was already way ahead of him on that. She had remained at the pub until about ten, and she probably would have stayed longer if he hadn't seen the dark circles under her eyes and insisted she go home and go to bed.

Surprisingly, while she was sound asleep, Seamus wasn't. The dog was wide awake and anxious, standing next to Mia on the bed. When he saw Padraig enter the room, the dog started to whine.

The cry and his high-alert demeanor sent a shot of adrenaline through Padraig, chasing away all traces of the exhaustion he'd been feeling.

They'd gotten Seamus from a rescue shelter. The brown and white pup was a Sheltie-Spitz mix and he had just turned eight months old. Padraig had jokingly proclaimed he and Seamus were kindred spirits, both one hundred percent under Mia's spell, devoted and in love with the sweet woman.

Although lately, he was starting to think the dog viewed him more as competition than owner. Padraig harbored no illusion that the dog was his. Seamus had chosen his "human" and there was no winning the puppy's affections with Mia around.

Mia had suffered a seizure a few days after they'd gotten Seamus back in July and since then, the dog seemed to have developed some sort of sixth sense about them.

Colm had been the first to notice. He and Kelli had come over for dinner a few weeks earlier and Seamus, who was typically running amok, as only a badly trained puppy could do, had been uncharacteristically subdued. He had planted himself at Mia's feet and would not be moved, even by the food Kelli kept trying to sneak him under the table.

Seamus's agitation had continued to grow until he'd finally started nudging against Mia's leg, trying to move her off the chair. Padraig made the comment the dog had developed the bad habit of pushing Mia every once in a while. Said it was as if Seamus was herding her, trying to get her to go where he wanted her.

When Colm asked if it was only Mia he acted like that with, and Padraig confirmed, Colm mentioned reading a story about seizure dogs. He said some dogs had a heightened sense that allowed them to almost predict when a seizure was coming. He mentioned some dogs lying on their owners to keep them down so they wouldn't fall and others moving their owners forcibly away from stairs.

Padraig and Mia started putting the pieces together and realized Seamus's anxiety always preceded a seizure. And that night confirmed it when Mia suffered a seizure shortly after Kelli and Colm left.

Padraig walked to the bed and petted Seamus on the head. "Easy, boy. I'm here. We'll take care of her," he whispered.

They didn't have long to wait. Mia's seizure struck only a few minutes later, her body convulsing roughly. Seamus lay next to her as Padraig made sure she didn't shake herself off the bed. The seizures came more and more frequently, but that didn't mean Padraig was used to them. They still terrified him, made him feel helpless and weak.

Mercifully, this one was short. Mia opened her confused, glazed eyes for only a few seconds before drifting back to sleep. Her face was paler these days and, while he tried to deny it, he could see she was losing weight.

No matter how hard he tried to freeze time, it kept slipping away from him, the days going faster, rather than slower.

Twelve days. They were twelve days away from Mia's birthday. From their wedding.

And while he longed for October with every fiber of his being, he also wished the day would never come. That they could live forever in an eternal September.

With Mia here. Always here. With him.

Once the seizure passed, Seamus settled down. However, he didn't relinquish his spot right next to Mia.

Padraig undressed and climbed in on his side of the bed, reaching over the dog to gently stroke Mia's hair. She didn't stir.

Then his hand drifted to the dog. He gave Seamus a scratch between the ears. "Good boy," he murmured.

Seamus rolled toward him, and for the first time ever, snuggled next to Padraig. He couldn't figure out if the dog was offering or seeking comfort, but Padraig decided it didn't matter. The warmth of the dog's nearness soaked into him, chasing away the cold fear coursing through him.

Padraig lay there for nearly half an hour, stroking the puppy's soft fur, his gaze locked on Mia's face. It was becoming his standard nighttime routine. Watching as she slept, checking her face for pain, making sure her chest was still rising and falling steadily.

Seamus sighed heavily, distracting him. When Padraig looked at him, Seamus nuzzled more firmly against him.

"What are we going to do without her?" he whispered to the dog.

Seamus licked the hand petting him, and Padraig smiled even as a tear slid down his cheek. The dog shifted higher on the bed, burrowing under Padraig's arm. It honest to God felt as if the puppy was giving him a hug.

"Yeah," Padraig said with a sad chuckle. "I guess we'll just have to take care of each other, huh?"

The dog's eyes remained on his face for a few moments more before they closed slowly, his steady, even breathing lulling Padraig into sleep as well. Seamus's calmness reassured him that it was safe to look away for a little while and give in to the exhaustion.

Chapter Sixteen

October 2

Padraig stood near the bar, waiting for Aunt Keira to come downstairs and give them the signal it was time for the wedding to begin.

He'd been holding his breath, praying for this day ever since Mia had accepted his marriage proposal in June. When September rolled around, he started to believe in miracles.

Mia's headaches were still there, growing more frequent, and sometimes brutally painful. She was averaging two to three seizures a week, and lately it was becoming difficult for her to remember things. The pain made her nauseous, so she'd lost weight. They'd had to do a quick fix to her wedding dress a few nights ago because it had gotten too big on her.

Padraig was taking more and more time off from work, not wanting to leave her alone in the apartment on nights when she wasn't well enough to come to the pub with him. His family and Kelli had been there for them every step of the way, either covering his shifts at the bar or taking turns staying with Mia. He couldn't imagine doing any of this without them.

He glanced around the room. This wedding was a perfect example of how amazing they were. They'd closed the pub today for the ceremony, and at six a.m., his aunts, uncles and cousins had converged, taking the building from sports bar to elegant wedding venue in hours.

The place looked amazing, decorated in an array of fall flowers and yellow roses and cream tulle. They'd moved tables so that they could have a proper altar and seating area, as well as an aisle for Mia to walk down with Pop Pop.

He could see Riley scurrying around on Sunday's Side, doing some last-minute setting up for the reception/birthday party following the ceremony.

Colm walked over, reaching out to straighten Padraig's bowtie. "You clean up good, bro. Of course, I could have told you you'd rock a tux. Because I do."

Padraig laughed. "Looking forward to meeting the woman who gets *you* dressed up in a monkey suit."

"I'm not in a hurry for that. Enjoying my bachelorhood too much. I'm more than happy to let you play the pussy-whipped-hubby role."

"Keep talking, Colm. It's only going to make things more fun for me when you fall fast and hard."

"You spend too much time talking to Pop Pop. He's got you convinced we've got some sort of genetic flaw."

"I don't think Pop Pop views it as a flaw."

"You guys ready?" Kelli asked, gesturing toward the door that led to the Collins Dorm upstairs. "Keira just ducked her head out and gave us the thumbs-up."

Padraig took a deep breath, marveling at his complete lack of nerves. He'd always heard weddings were stressful events, where the bride and groom typically suffered from cold feet in the minutes just before the vows. If anything, the only thing Padraig was anxious for was the end of the ceremony. The part where Kelli would tell him he could kiss his bride. Because it would mean Mia was his. Finally.

He, Colm and Finn took their places near the makeshift altar that Kelli stood in front of. She leaned over to whisper, "I knew I'd find a way to stand next to you when you got married. This is a hundred times better than best man."

"No, it's not," Colm contradicted. "I'm way more important here."

Kelli rolled her eyes. "In your dreams."

Padraig chuckled, but the sound was cut short when Hunter began to play the guitar. Mia had freaked when she'd found out Hunter, Teagan and Sky had volunteered to play the processional, as well as perform at the reception. The three of them had been out on the road, touring the past few months, along with his cousin Ailis. He'd been thrilled when they were able to rearrange their concert schedule so they could be here.

He'd left the choice of song she'd walk down the aisle to up to Mia, unsurprised when she chose "My Heart Will Go On." Teagan took lead on the singing, Sky providing background vocals.

His family didn't do anything small, which meant Mia wasn't without plenty of bridesmaid options. In the end, it was decided Sunnie and Yvonne would do the honors, with Yvonne serving as maid of honor. Mia had grown closest to Sunnie and Yvonne, the three of them nearly the same age.

Padraig suspected if Kelli hadn't already claimed the officiant role, Mia actually would have asked *her* to be maid of honor. The two of them had a standing brunch date every Sunday. They'd become thick as thieves, and Padraig had actually suffered a pang or two of jealousy over how close they'd grown.

As Yvonne and Sunnie took their places next to them at the altar, all eyes turned toward the back.

Pop Pop appeared first, turning to offer Mia a hand as she descended the last step.

Padraig stopped breathing when she turned the corner in her simple white, off-the-shoulder dress. She carried a bouquet of white and yellow roses, and she'd opted for leaving her hair down, adorning it with a short wisp of a veil at the back.

"Wow," Colm whispered.

Padraig smiled, his eyes filling with tears. "She's beautiful."

Pop Pop looked every inch the proud grandfather as he walked with Mia on his arm, beaming as they passed all the friends and family in attendance. Mia's boss, Phyllis, had flown in from Chicago, and they'd invited Dr. Richards. The rest of the guests were his family and close friends, as well as some regular patrons from the pub. Most of the people had known him longer, but they'd come to love Mia dearly as well.

Once they reached the front, Pop Pop gave her a quick kiss on the cheek, then turned around and gave Padraig a hug as well, whispering, "I'm so proud of you, boy. You picked a good one."

Padraig swallowed hard, trying to dislodge the lump growing in his throat. He still had vows to get through. He was struggling to beat down the emotions as he swiped at his eyes. One look told him Mia was fighting the same tears.

Pop Pop claimed his seat in the front row next to Padraig's mom, Lane, then he and Mia turned toward Kelli.

"Mawwiage is what bwings us togethaw today," Kelli said, arms uplifted, doing a spot-on imitation of the priest in *The Princess Bride*.

212

They all laughed, and just like that, Kelli had found a way to break the heaviness of the moment, to remind Padraig that today was a happy one, meant to be filled with family, laughter and cake.

She winked at him before continuing…in her own voice. "We're here today to celebrate the marriage and love of Padraig and Mia. Helen Keller once said, 'The best and most beautiful things in this world cannot be seen or even heard, but must be felt with the heart.' I believe all of us in this room have been witnesses to that love as we've watched Mia and Padraig together these past few months."

Kelli went on to read a poem and say a few more words. Padraig had a hard time concentrating on what she was saying, his mind whirring over too many other things. Too many emotions were crashing in on him at once.

He jerked when Kelli said, "Today, Padraig and Mia have written their own vows to each other."

Kelli gestured to Padraig, who started to reach for the piece of paper in his coat pocket, but then he stopped and left it there. He had the words memorized. Hell, they were written in Sharpie marker on his heart.

He turned to face the most stunning bride in history. She handed her bouquet to Yvonne, allowing him to take her hands in his.

"Mia, I didn't know who I was in March. I thought I knew. Thought I was Padraig Collins, Paddy to my family and friends. I had a great job, a great family, a great life." He paused. "Or at least, that's what I thought…until I met you. You opened my eyes to a new reality. To the world. I never realized up until that point, I had blinders on; that I was failing to see so many things that were right in front of me. They fell away that night in March. When you walked in, sat down at the bar, and changed it all. For the first time in his life, this stupid, blind man saw everything."

Mia sniffled and Kelli reached into her sleeve, pulling out a tissue for the bride and one for herself.

Padraig continued, aware of the cracks and breaks in his voice as he struggled to get the words out. "You've taught me how to live, how to dream. You've filled my life with adventure and laughter. Every single day I say, this is it, I can't love her any more than I do at this minute. Then I wake up the next day and fall even deeper. You are my life, Mia. Everything I've ever wanted. My funny Tilly Mint. My perfect Beauty. And I will love you until the day I die."

He lifted her hands to place a quick kiss on her knuckles. Then he noticed Kelli handing out another tissue. He glanced back just in time to see Colm wiping his eyes too. The four of them shared a quick laugh at their endless waterworks. Thank God he was surrounded by these people. They kept reeling him in, grounding him, getting him through the happiest—and God, the saddest—day of his life.

Because as much as he wanted this to be only about them, their wedding, their love, he couldn't shake the knowledge that time was running out.

Mia took a deep breath, and he admired the steadiness of her voice. "You've got it all backwards. It's *you* who've given me everything, Paddy. I've lived a lot of my life alone. Always thought that was the way I preferred it. Until that day in March. You don't realize what true loneliness is until you sit in a doctor's office, find out that you're dying, then leave the place, knowing you don't have anyone to talk to."

She sucked in a ragged breath and quickly swiped away a tear. "But I haven't been alone since that day. You saw me, you followed me, you saved me." Mia paused, and he watched her try to pull it together. He squeezed her hands, reminding her he was still there.

Her gaze lifted and she smiled through the tears, then finished her vows the same way he had. "You're my life, Padraig. Everything I could ever want and more. You're my wonderful, wicked Beast. And I'm going to love you every day until…until I die."

Padraig pulled her into his embrace, holding her. Kelli gave them a moment to compose themselves, then she looked over at Colm.

"Rings," she said softly.

Padraig released Mia and the two of them exchanged rings, more promises, and then the sweetest kiss he'd ever received.

The moment they broke apart, they were surrounded. It was only then that Padraig realized there wasn't a dry eye in the place. He hugged his crying mother and aunts, got a strong man-hug from his dad, who had to clear his throat before he could say, "I'm so happy for you, son."

After that, the day seemed to switch into fast-forward as they hopped from one tradition to the next.

Colm and Yvonne offered toasts to the bride and groom before they dug into Riley's amazing spread. Then, afterwards, Riley pushed out two cakes.

One was a chocolate birthday cake that said "For Mia ONLY!" The second was a gorgeous wedding cake.

Mia laughed when she read the words on the cake. "No fork?"

Padraig shook his head. "Nope. Dig in."

She looked around the room, then seemed to realize his family was in on the joke. She didn't waste a minute, grabbing up a huge handful of the cake and taking a bite. There was chocolate all around her mouth as everyone sang "Happy Birthday" to her. Natalie was standing close enough to the cake table for Mia to hear her voice above the rest. She gave Padraig a horrified look, and they both laughed.

The wedding cake was served, and then Teagan and Sky made their way back to the stage.

Padraig took her hand, and they shared their first dance as Teagan and Sky gave a much better rendition of "Endless Love" than the karaoke one he and Mia had attempted.

Then the party kicked into overdrive. He and Mia remained on the floor, slow dancing, fast dancing, line dancing, chicken dancing.

When the clock hit midnight, Padraig decided it was time to pack it in. Though Mia was obviously willing to stay until dawn, he'd caught her rubbing her brow and trying to hide her winces of pain too many times in the past hour.

They said their goodbyes as the family lined the street and tossed birdseed, then they made their way back to the apartment.

Padraig helped her out of her dress, and she helped him peel off the tuxedo.

Naked, they climbed into bed. Seamus was already there, sound asleep at the foot of the mattress.

He reached for her, pulling her head against his chest.

"We're married," he said, not quite able to shake the sheer wonder of it. He'd married Mia Curtis, the love of his life.

She lifted her head, and they kissed. In the past few months, they'd shared countless kinds of kisses, passionate ones, friendly ones, comforting ones. This one felt the most genuine, the most true.

"It was the perfect night," he murmured, turning toward her as he rose to cage her beneath him. "And now it's time…"

She nodded and smiled. "For the perfect ending."

Mari Carr

Epilogue

March 28

Padraig followed Pop Pop into his living space at Aunt Riley's house blindly, and his grandfather stopped to raise a window, letting in the early spring breeze. "Surprisingly warm for March."

Padraig nodded, thinking he preferred the cold, biting wind of the previous year's March. It fit his mood better. "Yeah."

"It was a lovely memorial, son."

Padraig swallowed heavily. "It was."

The rest of the family was scattered about Riley's house, in the living room, dining room, kitchen. Some of the men were sipping scotch out on the screened-in back porch. Pop Pop had pulled him aside a few minutes earlier and asked him to join him in his room.

Padraig was grateful for the chance to escape. He was struggling to hold it together, and while Colm and Kelli meant well, if they gave him one more reassuring pat or smile, he was going to lose his shit and punch something. Or someone. He didn't doubt for a second that Colm would stand still for the hit if he really needed to take a swing.

His fists clenched and unclenched as he tried to swallow down the anger, the despair.

Pop Pop pointed to a chair. "Steady, boy. Have a seat."

He did as directed, numbly watching as Pop Pop poured a glass of Jameson for both of them. When Pop Pop returned, he claimed the seat next to him and handed him a glass. His grandfather lifted his in a silent toast before taking a sip.

Padraig merely stared at the amber liquid. He and Colm had fallen into an entire bottle of whiskey a few nights ago. It hadn't helped. Not even a little bit.

Mia had passed away in her sleep two weeks earlier. Given the pain she'd suffered since New Year's, Padraig was grateful the actual ending had been relatively peaceful. He'd crawled in next to her on the hospital bed they'd moved into their bedroom over Valentine's weekend and held her as she took her last breath.

She hadn't wanted a funeral, but had requested a simple memorial service with just the family. Padraig had chosen to hold it today, March twenty-eighth, a year to the day since Mia walked into the pub and changed his life.

"Take a drink of the bourbon, Paddy. Let it warm your insides, lad. Then the two of us are going to have a talk."

Padraig wanted to refuse, wanted to ask if they could just sit here together in the quiet. He was out of words. He was out of...everything.

Pop Pop lay a hand on his arm. "Drink."

He lifted the glass and took a longer swig than he probably should have. Pop Pop was right about the heat. The burn as the liquor slid down his throat did warm him up.

"I'm not going to ask how you're doing," Pop Pop began, "because I know. You're alternating between numb and pissed."

Padraig nodded slowly.

"Yeah. I've been there. I get it."

Something in his grandfather's tone told him the old guy really did understand. Of course, he'd walked a mile in these shoes. It might have been nearly fifty years ago, but it didn't appear time had weakened that memory.

"How did you do it, Pop Pop? How did you get over her?"

Pop Pop studied his face as if surprised by the question. "You're asking the wrong thing. You're never going to get over her. Never. What you have to do is get over *this*. The death part."

Padraig didn't see that happening. He'd had an entire year to prepare himself for this. This morning, he'd woken up, put on his Sunday best and realized he'd been a jackass.

There was no way to prepare for death.

"I can see you think I'm off my rocker," Pop Pop continued when Padraig didn't respond. "Focus on the life, son. You and Mia may not have had a long love, but you had a true one."

He nodded. The greatest love. "It was the best year of my life. And the worst."

"That's life, isn't it? Nothing is ever constant, nothing stays the same. If possible, perhaps you can find comfort in the fact that you're not alone. Every single person on this planet has experienced the same things as you. Every last one of us will feel love, anger, hate, sorrow, fear, loneliness, friendship...before our time is up. Every one of us gets it all. The whole enchilada."

Padraig grinned briefly, just a quick upturn of his lips before they fell again. "She told me not to be sad. Said it to me every damn day there at the end. Told me she was dying without a single regret. That her life had been perfect because she'd found me."

Padraig's voice broke, but he continued. "She made my life perfect, Pop Pop. And now I'm not sure how to go back to...God, fuck me...*nothing*. There's nothing now." He wiped his eyes, his chest tight with pain.

Pop Pop put his hand on Padraig's arm again, his grip tight for a man of ninety-three. "You don't have nothing. Son, you have everything. I know it doesn't feel like that now, but you have your family, your friends, people who care about you and who are going to help you get through this. More than that, you have Mia." Pop Pop leaned over and tapped Padraig on the chest. "You will carry that woman inside your heart every day until the second you breathe your last. Not a day has gone by in the last fifty years that I haven't thought about Sunday. I can hear her voice, see her smile, feel her presence."

"I just...miss her."

"Paddy, if I'd known how my life with Sunday would end, if I'd known she would die so young, I still would have married her, still would have had this incredible family with her. Would you change what *you* did?"

"What?" Padraig asked.

"If it were a year ago, and Mia walked into the pub and told you about her illness, knowing what you know now, would you have followed her?"

"Jesus. Of course I would!"

"Then you have to do this part too. You spent the last year, trying to ensure that beautiful girl died with no regrets. It's time for you to follow in her footsteps.

Do your grieving. Cry, scream, punch, get drunk. Do whatever you have to do...and then move on. Open up the blinds, let the sunshine in, and live. To do otherwise would be disrespectful to Mia's memory."

Padraig took another sip of whiskey, certain he'd never succeed at any of that. "Okay."

Pop Pop narrowed his eyes, studying his face. "Don't just say okay to shut the old man up. Say okay because you mean it."

Padraig grinned, and this time it stuck around five whole seconds before vanishing again. "I mean it."

Pop Pop didn't let him off quite that easy, looking at him for another full minute before he seemed convinced Padraig wasn't lying.

"Good. Here. I want to show you something." Pop Pop stood up and walked over to the wall that held all his beloved family photos. Padraig followed him. Each child and grandchild was represented there, the photos changing whenever Pop Pop found a more recent one that struck his fancy. Each frame was stuffed full, the new pictures going in on top of the old. One time, Padraig had taken his own frame down, opening it to flip through his life as seen through his grandfather's eyes.

He grew from a chubby baby to a toothless eight-year-old, holding up the first fish he'd ever caught. There was one of him peeking out from under the hood of his first car, grinning from ear to ear as he tried to fix the piece of shit. There was one of him, Colm and Kelli standing on the football field right after graduation, their gowns hanging open and loose, the three of them looking like they owned the world, now that they had those diplomas in their hands.

Pop Pop pointed to the wall, to Padraig's spot, and he saw that his frame held a new picture—and the sight of it took his breath away.

"Your mom took it last summer," Pop Pop said. "You were helping your dad plant trees, and Mia went along for the ride."

In the photo, he was shirtless, and he had just come inside to cool off for a few minutes. Mia had given him a glass of lemonade and he'd kissed the top of her head. He didn't realize his mother had taken the picture, didn't know that she'd caught them in that unguarded moment.

Padraig understood why his grandfather had chosen to hang this picture. It reflected the love and the friendship they'd shared. Looking at it made him smile, because he could almost smell the strawberry scent of her hair from her favorite shampoo, the way he'd remarked on how sweet she was. He remembered the way she'd giggled after that kiss, telling him his beard tickled.

Seamus had been standing between them, though he wasn't in the picture. They hadn't had the dog very long at that point, but he'd already become completely devoted to Mia. And jealous whenever Padraig got too close to "his human."

Padraig hadn't had the heart to leave the sweet dog home alone today. A quick glance out the window confirmed Finn was entertaining Seamus outside, playing a game of fetch with a tennis ball.

It broke his heart every time Seamus ran to the bedroom in search of Mia. He knew only too well how hard it was to forget for just a second she wasn't there, to walk in a room to tell her something, only to discover the bed was empty.

"You were lucky to find her, lad."

Padraig nodded. Lucky was right. "Yeah. I was."

"Here." Pop Pop handed him a box. It was wrapped in plain brown paper. "Mia asked me to pass this along to you after... Well, just after."

Padraig shook his head, unable to lift his hand to claim the present. "I don't...think..."

"Take it, son. I know what's in it. Mia showed me. You need to see it too."

He accepted the package, returning to his previous seat. Pop Pop followed.

Padraig opened the box and pulled apart the tissue paper. On top was an envelope with Mia's handwriting. It simply said, "Paddy." Beneath it was a book.

He opened the envelope first, his hand shaking as he pulled out the single sheet of paper.

My dearest Padraig.
My beloved husband.
Don't forget to dream big.
Always yours,
Mia

He didn't bother to wipe away the tears as he lifted the book and opened it. It was a scrapbook, and on the first page, Mia had titled it, *The Book of Dreams Come True.*

He flipped through the pages, smiling, even laughing through his tears as he looked at the photos Mia had selected. Each page contained the name of the dream and then a photograph of them doing it. There was a selfie they'd taken in front of the Hogwarts castle, one of them at Sacré-Coeur, another of their karaoke duet. Page after page was filled with reminders of his most perfect year. It truly had been the year all his dreams had come true.

The last picture was of the two of them on their wedding day, their faces covered with chocolate cake, both of them laughing.

Mari Carr

He ran his finger over the photograph, touching her face, wishing for the millionth time that she was still there.

"Turn the page," Pop Pop said.

Padraig did so, surprised to find more. He thought the wedding picture was the last.

On the pages following, Mia had listed the rest of the dreams, sans photos.

They were *his* dreams.

There was a page for the Super Bowl, the Stanley Cup, the World Series, then, because she loved to tease him, she'd added spots for March Madness, the U.S. Open, the Tour de France, and a NASCAR race.

Mia had recalled all his dreams, including the Grand Canyon, the cruise to Mexico, the marathon, fishing and the Appalachian Trail. She'd even added, "Trip to Ireland with Pop Pop."

The last two pages were reserved for "True Love, part two" and "Paddy's Little Girl."

He gripped the edges of the book tightly—and for several minutes, he let himself fall apart.

Pop Pop didn't say anything. He simply reached over and put his hand on his shoulder, let him know he was there. Pop Pop had always been there.

After a while, he was able to pull himself together. Pop Pop handed him a hanky and Padraig wiped off his face.

Taking a deep breath, he looked up. He wasn't quite sure how to explain it, but somehow the book grounded him, given him a purpose.

"There's my lad," Pop Pop said with a smile. "Mia's given you a job to do. Are you going to let her down?"

Padraig shook his head. "No. It's funny...I know we spent so much of this past year dealing with the fact that she was dying, but when I look back on it, all I can remember is how much Mia taught me about living. I can't shut down, Pop Pop. Can't stop moving. I'm never going to stop loving her."

"I know. But that's the beauty of being alive. We can love as many people as we want to."

Padraig glanced down and ran his hand over the cover of the book. For the first time in weeks, he managed a genuine smile. "She made a hell of a list for me."

Pop Pop chuckled. "Then I guess you'd better get busy."

Dear Reader,

I was warned not to write this book by pretty much everyone: my author friends, my beta readers, my family. I was told this wasn't a romance, and that there was a good chance I would lose some long-time readers. I genuinely believe this *is* a romance novel. So obviously, I wrote the book anyway. I couldn't *not* write it, because these characters wouldn't leave me alone. The story wouldn't go away because so many of the things Padraig and Mia struggled with are things that have kept me up more than a few nights the past couple of years.

I turned 48 this year. I don't consider that old. Honestly, as the years go by, I swear I actually feel younger. However, there have been several "moments" in my life lately that have made me begin to think more closely about life, death, regrets, and love.

There are several themes in this story, things that have begun to come clearer to me as I've watched loved ones deal with serious health concerns, and as I've tried to face some of my own fears about death.

Love doesn't stop when someone discovers they're dying. If anything, love seems to be the one thing that grows stronger, rings out more truly, because people become less afraid to say how they feel. Why is it so hard to look at those we care about on an ordinary, *nothing's happening* Wednesday and say, "I love you" or "You matter to me" or "You make my life better"? Those words shouldn't be reserved for times when we fear we're losing the ones we love. They should be spoken every day...without reservation.

Life is too short to hide who you truly are. Padraig commented to Mia that now was the time to be real, to reveal to the world who she truly was. There is a

227

freedom in feeling comfortable enough to say, "This is me. Warts and all." Life is hard enough. Wearing a mask and pretending to be someone we aren't only adds to the struggle.

You want to know who I am? I'm an overweight, middle-aged wife and mother who drinks way too much wine, curses her ever-growing curves and spends too many nights wide awake suffering from panic attacks she can't explain. But I also have a good sense of humor, and I think I'm a pretty solid friend. No one cries (or drinks) alone in my presence! In the story, Kelli talked about the yin and the yang in life. I suspect we all have things we love and hate about ourselves. You know what? Own them—the good and the bad. They're there and they're yours.

Live every day like you're dying. Don't assume there's going to be a tomorrow or a next week or a next year. I have a motto I like to live by. If I'm going to die tomorrow, I'm going to be full and hungover (hence those ever-growing curves). Padraig and Mia planned the dream trips, they took the long drive to the ocean on a whim, they sang karaoke—loud and off-key. They unplugged from computers and phones and spent quality time with family and friends. They found time to do the things that make life worth living. So many of the things on Mia's list are also on mine. And I have been working my way through them, determined that I won't have any regrets at the end.

Happily ever after doesn't have to mean forever. One of the main things that bothered my friends when I talked about this book was the fact that Mia dies at the end. To them, that meant the story didn't have a traditional happily ever after. I disagree. Mia and Padraig found a very true and meaningful love. Dying young is sad—dying alone is tragic. Mia didn't die alone. She died in the arms of a man who adored her, who gave her his whole heart unconditionally. If that's not a happy ending, then I guess I don't know what is.

It all boils down to this: I hope this story touched you in some way. That it makes you think, allows you to appreciate your blessings, encourages you to take an impromptu trip somewhere fun just because you want to and you can. And in the end, I hope you will indulge this author for her unconventional view of life and what constitutes a happy ending. Because I will always believe those who have lived well, laughed often and loved deeply have already found their happily ever after.

Always,
Mari

**"*Laughter through tears is my favorite emotion.*" –
Dolly Parton**

With that in mind...

Wild Devotion Frequently Asked Questions
...that haven't been asked yet
(I'm being proactive)

Q: What the hell did you just do?
A: I'm going to assume that's a rhetorical question and move on.

Q: Is Padraig going to get another story?
A: Yes. He is.

Q: Are you going to give him a happy ending that lasts more than five minutes?
A: Probably.

Q: Have you lost your freaking mind?
A: Rhetorical again, right?

Q: Do you seriously expect me to buy the next Wilder Irish book after this?
A: I sincerely hope you will. Does it help if I say the next one is a full-fledged romantic comedy (think *Saturday Night Special*)?

Q: That depends...whose story is next?
A: Fiona, Teagan and Sky's youngest daughter.

Q: Is it a ménage? Because that might be the only way I forgive you.

A: No, but there *will* be a couple of ménage stories in the Wilder Irish series. So see? You should totally stick around!

Q: Are you planning to kill anyone else?
A: Not right away. LOL—just kidding! Sort of.

Enjoy *Wild Devotion*?

Please consider leaving a review.

Mari Carr

Enjoy this excerpt from Wild at Heart, Wilder Irish, book 4. Available now.

Chapter One

"You sure you're doing okay?" Fiona asked again.

Padraig gave her a grin that seemed like a shadow of his former one. "I'm sure, Fee. Honest."

She nodded and took his words at face value, praying they were the truth. Padraig's beloved wife, Mia, had passed away a couple of weeks earlier. Her memorial service had been two days ago and since then, the entire family had joined forces to keep him busy, to make sure he didn't feel alone in his grief.

Fiona had only met Mia a handful of times over the year she and Padraig had been married, but she'd adored the upbeat, lovely woman. She'd invited Padraig to join her for lunch at her family's bar, Pat's Pub. They were currently on Sunday's Side, indulging in massive cheeseburgers and fries.

"Pop Pop said you're taking some time off," she said.

Padraig nodded. "Yeah. I'm heading to Uncle Aaron's cabin on the Shenandoah River for a week. Taking Seamus for long walks in the woods and doing some fishing. Kind of looking forward to getting away."

"I suspect it'll be Seamus taking you for walks. That dog is wild."

Padraig chuckled. "Yeah. Probably should sign him up for obedience school, but I've kind of gotten used to his hijinks. Not sure I want to make him boring, well-behaved, and trained like all the other dogs in the world.

"You really want to go away? By yourself?" Fiona couldn't understand how that would be helpful. She thrived in the presence of people and hated being alone.

Padraig rearranged the fries on his plate...again. He was playing with his food more than eating it. She tried not to notice that he'd obviously lost some weight since the holidays. The new year had not been kind to him.

"I love this family, Fee, and everything everyone has done for me the past few months, but I need a break. I walk in a room and everyone stops laughing and starts talking quieter, like I can't handle happiness anymore. I don't blame anyone for that, I really don't, but I don't want everyone feeling like they have to change the way they feel and act to match me. I just had my guts ripped out. I'm the one who needs to figure out how to deal with that."

"Paddy," she started.

"Besides I can't be in the apartment without feeling Mia's presence there. Time is the only thing that's going to help, so I'm taking some for myself. Talked to Aunt Lauren about it and she didn't see any harm in getting away for a bit, coming back and starting fresh. I like the idea of that. There's a cycle of sadness looming over us here and we need to break it."

"If you get lonely, you only have to call. I can come visit. And I know Colm and Kelli and—"

"I'm going to be fine. Promise."

She reached across the table, took his hand and squeezed it. "I'm going to hold you to that."

He grinned and this time it felt more genuine, more like the real Padraig. "I wouldn't worry about me extending my week's vacation. Gonna have to get back in time to watch you and your friends film that show. Want my cameo."

Fiona laughed. Six months earlier, she'd arranged to have the season finale of *Wild Winters* filmed at Pat's Pub. After graduating from college, she and her best friends, Asher, Owen and Teddy had decided to try to shop the sitcom they'd written as a lark during their senior year at USC. Each of them had made some connections during their tenure at the university with people in the business and one phone call led to another that led to a meeting, and before she knew it, *Wild Winters* was on the air and a weekly staple. People were calling it *Seinfeld* for Millennials and it had taken over the number one spot halfway during the second year of production.

She was living a dream life, her days spent surrounded by her best friends, living on coffee and donuts as they laughed their asses off, trying to out-joke each other. With the show's continued success, the list of famous people who wanted cameos or even recurring bit parts had grown and she had actually walked down the red carpet the last two years, climbing up the stairs to the stage to accept an Emmy for Outstanding Writing in a Comedy series with the guys.

Pop Pop told her she lived under a lucky star and she believed him. She was twenty-five years old and her life rocked.

It was actually Owen and Asher who'd suggested filming the season finale in Baltimore at her family's pub. They'd come up with a great gag that was tailored made for an East Coast trip to the Irish pub. Owen's first trip to the pub had been for Thanksgiving their sophomore year in college during the three minutes the two of them had actually dated.

Ever since, he'd always found a way to finagle an invite back, claiming he couldn't survive a year that didn't include Aunt Riley's turkey and dressing. Of course, he wasn't the only "extra" sitting around the

Thanksgiving table. Once someone was unofficially "adopted" into the Collins family, they were in for life. Asher had come home with her the last few summers for long weekends just to get away from the hubbub of Hollywood. He was also very quickly indoctrinated into the family, so she shouldn't have been surprised when they hit her up with the idea of filming in the pub. They loved the place as much as she did.

Her family had embraced the idea wholeheartedly and talked of nothing else since. Fiona had nearly canceled when Mia passed away, but Padraig and Pop Pop had both vetoed that decision, insisting that the show go on. She was a bit worried that was why Padraig was clearing out and the reason she'd asked him to lunch. If he said having the show here would bother him, she was pulling the plug no matter what anyone else said.

"You're sure your decision to leave isn't because of the show?"

Padraig narrowed his eyes. "I'm only saying this one more time, Fiona. You have to film that show here. For one thing, it would be huge for business and for another, it's going to give everyone else the same break I'm trying to get. I haven't been the only one hurting these past few months. I'm grateful to have you and your friends here. Filming that sitcom will give everyone something good, something fun, to focus on for a little while. They need that. They deserve that after all they've done for me."

She sighed and accepted his words. "Okay." She smiled and squeezed his hand tighter. "Okay," she repeated.

He squeezed her hand back, then released it to take a sip of his soda.

"Actually, you're probably smart to escape this week. The producer is calling for some last-minute rewrites and setting up the cameras and doing the blocking is going to be tedious as hell. The majority of the cast isn't even showing up until the week you get back. Not to mention, I've gotta try to deal with the ultimate diva himself, Owen Winters. Ever since he won that second Emmy for Best Actor in a Comedy, he's been impossible to live with."

Padraig feigned shock. "What? Owen? A diva? No way. Playboy maybe, but diva?"

"The man is a menace."

Her cousin wasn't fooled by her words. "He's been one of your best friends since freshman year at USC. You would have dumped him seven years ago if that was really the case."

"I did dump him. Sophomore year. He's like herpes. Keeps coming back."

Padraig tilted his head and lifted one shoulder, a sure sign he was about to start teasing her. "The way Owen tells it, he dumped you."

"We dated for three minutes. That was all the time I needed to know he wasn't my type."

Padraig chuckled. "In truth, Fee, I've always thought Owen was your type, more than that Brock guy anyway."

Fiona glanced around the restaurant. No one was nearby, so she decided to come clean. "Brock and I broke up."

"Good." It was a simple, one word answer that confirmed she was right to start breaking this news with Padraig.

Fiona giggled. "Yeah. It is."

"It was long overdue. The two of you were apart more than together and it never sounded like your paths

238

were headed in the same direction. Can I add that I hope you dumped him?"

Her grin grew. "I did. I totally did. In February."

"Man. I guess I am out of the loop if I'm just now hearing about it."

She shook her head. "You're not. Actually, you are the loop. I haven't told anyone else."

"Why not?"

Fiona shrugged. "I wanted to make sure it stuck this time."

"Will it?" Padraig asked.

She didn't hesitate to nod. "It's sticking."

"Good," Padraig repeated. "So it's time for you to find a nice guy. Owen—"

She scowled. "No way. He has an overinflated opinion of himself. Trust me when I say, no one will ever love Owen more than he loves himself."

"Me thinks she doth protest too much."

"Wow, Paddy. You're a regular poet. Come up with that all on your own?"

"Then what about that other fella? Asher. He's a nice guy."

Fiona grinned at her cousin's attempts at matchmaking. "He's very nice. However, we've drifted too far over the line in our relationship. He's like a brother to me. I know too much about him and he knows *way* too much about me."

"You're protesting again."

Fiona rolled her eyes and growled.

Padraig winked at her and they started eating again. She was delighted when he picked up his burger and actually took a big bite. Hope emerged. Padraig was going to be okay.

"Whoa, Fee. You might wanna take it easy on the grease there," Owen said, hip tapping her over in the booth, so he could sit down and grab a couple fries from her plate.

Owen was terrible at greetings, something she constantly gave him shit for. He'd come in, interrupt whatever was happening with a conversation of his own choosing, then realize several minutes in, he hadn't even said hello. They'd actually written that habit into the show as a running gag and it always got a lot of laughs.

"Get your own," she said, tugging her plate away.

Owen ignored her and continued stealing fries.

"So you guys made it to Baltimore, huh? Asher and Teddy here?" she asked. The last time she'd seen Owen had been nearly a week ago...in California.

"Yeah. We got to the hotel about an hour ago. They're unpacking."

"Owen," Padraig said, reaching out to shake his hand. "It's good to see you again."

"Oh yeah. Hey, Paddy. You too, man. I'm fucking starving. Food on the plane was shit." Owen pushed Fiona's hands away easily, grabbing her burger and helping himself to two big bites before returning it to the plate.

She leaned back and sighed. Owen thought with three things: his dick, his stomach and then his brain, which was a distant third in the lineup. She shoved the rest of her lunch toward him. "Here. I don't want it anymore. It has your boy cooties on it."

Owen reached over her for the salt and vinegar, pouring each on the fries before digging in with gusto. And that was when the light went on and Owen realized he'd forgotten to say hello. He put the food down and focused on her cousin. "Damn. I'm sorry about that. How are you doin', P? I've been thinking about you a lot."

"I'm hanging in there."

"I was really sorry to hear about Mia. She was awesome. The best."

Padraig nodded a quick *thanks*. "She was." Then he quickly changed the subject. "Fiona tells me you have a couple busy weeks ahead of you."

Owen, bless him, took the subject switch in stride, recognizing the fact Padraig didn't want to talk about his loss. "Same shit, different coast. Going to be cool filming the finale here in the pub. Nice of your family to let us take over like this."

"Pop Pop is beside himself, really excited about it. Been practicing that line you've given him for weeks. Starting to remind me of that old *Seinfeld* gag with all his different renditions. 'These pretzels are making me thirsty.'"

They laughed as Padraig wiped his mouth and glanced around. "Guess I better start saying my goodbyes. Want to get on the road by two, so I'm not trying to find my way to that cabin in the woods in the dark. Thanks for the company, Fee."

She nodded. "Gonna miss you. If you get bored, come back early, okay?"

"I'll be home in one week, ready to wow those cameras of yours with my bartending skills."

They all stood, Padraig giving her a hug, then shaking Owen's hand again. He headed toward the kitchen, starting his farewells with Riley.

Fiona studied Owen's appearance, aware that he'd done well to hide his identity on the walk from the hotel to the pub. Owen preferred the hipster-look and he was working it today. With his beard, toboggan, and colorful tats peeking out beneath the short sleeves of his dark gray T-shirt, strangers would probably pass him on the street assume he was a musician in a grunge band until they took a harder look and realized he was a TV star.

She sat back down and Owen followed her in, reclaiming the same spot. She pointed across the booth. "Other side is free now."

He leaned back, resting his arm along the bench seat, ignoring her. "Feels good to be back." Owen glanced around the restaurant. "Forgot how pretty the girls are in Baltimore. And on this coast, my fame and good looks seems more potent, you know what I mean? Less competition once I'm out of Hollywood."

"Is that the real reason you suggested filming in Baltimore? So you could hold the monopoly on TV star?"

He gave her a wink that was annoyingly charming, even though his words aggravated the shit out of her. "I like getting laid. It's going to be a busy month."

Sometimes she wondered why she hung out with Owen. When he started strutting and bragging about his fame or his sexual conquests, she was hard-pressed not to throat punch him.

"We're here to work, remember?"

Owen turned to face her and Fiona was forced to admit why his flirty nature never truly bothered her. He really was hot. And funny. And while he pretended to be a ladies' man, she suspected a lot of that was more bluster than truth.

"Work is play, you know that."

"I'm surprised you're okay with this trip. Thought you were in love with…what's her name?"

He chuckled "Ashley 4. It's over. She was a stage ten clinger."

Fiona rolled her eyes. "Of course. How could I forget that name?" She and the other guys had taken to numbering his girlfriends with the same name in an attempt to distinguish who exactly they were talking about. So far they'd had to tabulate up to four Ashleys, three Brittanys and two Amandas. "Do me a favor.

Next time you meet an Ashley, walk away. It hasn't been a good name for you."

"I'll keep that in mind, but I'm not making any promises. If she's got nice tits, I'm going for five."

"You're a pig."

He laughed. "You know I'm just trying to get a rise out of you. Why don't we text Teddy and Asher and tell them to bring their laptops and we'll work from here? Figure we can knockout the changes Al wanted better if we're in the pub."

Fiona made a buzzer noise to indicate he'd given the wrong answer. "Errrr. No. No work will happen in the pub because you'll start ordering pitchers, gossiping about Hollywood stars with Pop Pop and his cronies, and we'll all be three sheets to the wind before dusk."

As always, Owen ignored her and sent off the text. Teddy replied instantly that they would be there in five. Owen, Teddy and Asher were sharing a suite at a hotel just around the corner.

Fiona had opted for staying at the Collins Dorm above the pub while she was home, sleeping in Caitlyn and Ailis' old room. It had been dubbed the Collins Dorm by Aunt Riley when the younger generation began moving into the spacious apartment where their parents had lived with Pop Pop while growing up.

Unlike most of her cousins, Fiona had never lived in Baltimore, her childhood spent on a tour bus with her parents and Ailis. Fiona had always loved life on the move, a different city every night, while Ailis had been less fond of it.

The second Ailis graduated from high school, she set up camp in Baltimore, determined to make up for every second of the time she'd lost with the family while growing up. That decision lasted only a few years until her homebody sister fell in love with someone just like their dear old dad, Sky Mitchell. Which meant

Ailis was back on road, on another tour bus, with Hunter Maxwell. Hunter's star was on the rise and Fiona couldn't be happier for him. The guy was seriously talented, but more than that, he was just as head over heels for Ailis, as her sister was for him. They fit together perfectly and for the first time in her life, Fiona actually felt a bit jealous of her quiet, boring, responsible, dependable, sensible, snoozeville sister.

Her oldest cousin, Caitlyn had also moved out of the Dorm, opting to live with her uber-hot, billionaire boyfriend, Lucas Whiting, which meant there was an empty bedroom in the apartment for her to use.

Fiona had never felt the need to live near the family and was cool with just visiting from time to time. Baltimore was freaking cold in the winter and after four years of college in sunny California, she'd discovered she was made for heat, not snow.

But that didn't mean she didn't sometimes regret missing out on so much. Her family was, hands-down, the greatest, craziest, most fun crew in the world and there'd been too many Facetime conversations where she'd found herself jealous not to be in the same room.

She was in Baltimore for a month and Fiona intended to take advantage of that time, to immerse herself in a true Collins lifestyle.

Her cousin, Yvonne, came over to clear their table. "Hey Owen, when did you get here?"

"Just a few minutes ago. Good to see you again, Yvonne."

"Did you want to order anything?" she asked.

The asshole rubbed his full stomach, claiming he couldn't eat another bite. Fiona decided hitting the pub side probably wasn't such a bad thing. She was still hungry and in the mood for some of Aunt Riley's spicy shrimp appetizer. God, Owen wasn't wrong. Too long in Baltimore, around all this good cooking, and she was destined to gain fifty pounds. She'd have to take Yvonne up on her invitation to go running in the morning with her and her BFF, Leo.

"We're heading over to the pub side, waiting for the other guys so we can do some work," Owen said, rising from the booth, and reaching down to help her out. Fiona gave him a funny look, not used to his chivalry. Then she decided he was probably putting on a show for Yvonne. The guy was a master at charming women. Except her, of course. For one thing, she wasn't fooled by his act and for another, Owen had put her in the one-of-the-guy's category years ago. Right after their break up in college.

"Cool," Yvonne said. "Uncle Tris is working. He can set you up with drinks. I'll stop by once the other two get here and see if they want some food."

Owen gave Yvonne a smile and a wink and then they headed for a corner booth in the pub. Uncle Tris waved to indicate he'd seen them and would be over in a minute. The bar was relatively quiet right now, but Fiona knew that would change as soon as five o'clock hit and folks started heading in for their happy hours.

They hadn't been there a full minute before Teddy and Asher walked in, looking around for them. Owen gave them a wave. He'd claimed the seat next to her again, but she didn't bother to mention it since she knew the other guys were coming.

Asher slid in first, sitting across from her, as Teddy followed. She grinned as she watched both men do exactly what she expected. Asher pulled his laptop from the case, firing it up, clearly ready to get straight to work.

Meanwhile, Teddy's eyes had yet to land on anyone at the table. He was doing his usual scan of the room in search of available guys.

"Slim pickings," he murmured before catching a glimpse of Tris behind the bar. "Well hello, mountain man. I wouldn't mind taking a drink from your tap, Daddy."

Fiona crinkled her nose. "Um...gross. That's my uncle Tris, Teddy. He's very married and very straight."

Teddy sighed. "That's a loss for our side. No worries though. I've been exploring Tinder and while the Beach Boys might long for California girls, I'm not going to lie, Maryland has some very fine boys."

Asher pushed his glasses up on his nose, tsking quietly. He was the hottest nerd on the planet, something Fiona liked to tease him about. He was Clark Kent incarnate with his dark, clean cut hairstyle and black-rimmed glasses that did nothing to hide his ice blue eyes and only served to accentuate his strong jawline.

Fiona sighed. She really needed to stop looking at her best friends so closely. It did nothing to improve her current dateless, sexless, horny state.

"We're only here a few weeks, Teddy. Isn't it wrong to try to find someone on Tinder when you're not planning on sticking around? You'd be leading them on."

Teddy wrapped his arm around Asher's shoulders in a friendly manner, even as his face revealed something more like pity. "I always forget how young and innocent you are, my son. There's this little thing called a hookup, Ash. It's all about the three F's. Foreplay, forward thrusting and farewell. The only man I'd ever consider exploring the fourth F—forever—with is you and you refuse to come out of the closet."

Owen and Fiona both laughed as Asher closed his eyes in his typical praying-for-patience style. "I've told you a million times, Ted. I'm not gay."

Teddy shrugged his shoulder as if the words meant nothing. This joke was nothing new. In fact, in their little foursome of comedy writers, they probably shared no less than a hundred inside jokes and this one was the oldest.

Funny how it never really got old.

Teddy wiggled his eyebrows. "Come on, Ash. Come to the dark side. It's fun over here. We have lightsabers."

Asher, their eternal straight man—literally and figuratively—shook his head. "You, me and Owen have been roommates since freshman year of college. I've seen both of your lightsabers a thousand times. Believe me, neither one of them has tempted me to give up Princess Leia's buns."

"Hey," Owen said, "why you gotta drag me into this? My lightsaber is pretty spectacular. Tell him, Fee."

She shook her head. "You know the rule. When it turns to *Star Wars* puns, I'm out."

None of the men had a chance to complain.

"That reminds me." Asher handed something across the table to Fiona.

"What's this?" she asked when she recognized the material. "My sweater."

"You mentioned on the phone it was chillier in Baltimore than you expected, so I swung by your place to get it."

Fiona smiled, touched by the sweet gesture. "That was so nice of you."

Asher shrugged off the compliment, looking somewhat relieved to have her grateful attention distracted from him when Tris arrived.

"Hey Fiona, fellas." He looked at Teddy and Fiona did the introductions as he was the only one of her friends who hadn't been to the pub before.

"Uncle Tris, this is Teddy Martin, the other writer on the show. And you remember Owen Winters and Asher McCarthy, of course."

Tris shook all their hands. "Sure do." He gestured behind the bar to the framed signed headshot Owen had given Tris during his last visit. "Appreciate the picture, Owen. You got a lot of fans on this side of the country. They're always impressed when they hear my niece writes for *Wild Winters* and find out you've been in the bar before."

Owen preened. The guy loved hearing being famous. Way too much. "Yeah, well, I feel there's something I should confess, Tris. It's been weighing heavy on my mind for quite a while now and I think I need to come clean."

Fiona leaned back and resisted the urge to roll her eyes. Owen was about to launch into some big old pile of ridiculousness from his dramatic tone. The man truly was born to be an actor.

"Oh yeah?" Tris asked, with a slight grin.

"As you know, the first time I was here, Fee and I were only nineteen and on break from college. I was young and in love—"

Teddy pretended to cough, barking out the word, "lust," as he did so.

Tris snickered.

Owen continued as if nothing had happened. "I was an innocent boy really and I'm afraid I was led astray. Fiona insisted that we sneak down here in the middle of the night and steal a few shots of whiskey." He gestured toward her. "There wasn't anything I wouldn't do to impress her and, well...she made me do it. I told her it was wrong, but she wouldn't listen."

Fiona recalled that night very well. And everything he said was true. But the roles were reversed.

Tris laughed. "Yeah. That's our Fee. Bad to the bone."

She snorted at her uncle's joke.

"Just the same," Tris said, "I'll be sure to add those drinks to your tab tonight in order to help clear that conscience of yours, Owen."

Owen frowned. "But—"

"No, no," Tris said, well able to give as good as he got. "No more apologies. Nothing like cold, hard cash to absolve you of your sins."

"You sure he's straight?" Teddy asked Fiona, not bothering to hide his question from Tris. "No shot he's even a little gay?"

"No shot," Tris replied. "But my wife is stopping by later if you want to consult with her on that."

Teddy gave him a wink. "Well, if you ever change your mind…"

"You'll be the first man I call." Tris laughed.

Praise for Wild Devotion

"Like every good romance, this is a **celebration of love**, of its power to change us and move us and make our lives beautiful." ★★★★★ *Fedora, Goodreads*

"Did I cry? **Hell yes**. Did I laugh? **Yep**. Did I love? **You bet I did**." ★★★★★ *Katherine, Goodreads*

"It was **provocative, intense** … it was **beautiful** and **fun**. It made me smile, it made me cry, it made my heart full and then broke it." ★★★★★ *Kitty Angel, Goodreads*

"Believe me, you will laugh, you will cry **and you will want to hug every single character** in this story and then maybe cry some more, but once I turned the last page, I cried again because the story had ended." ★★★★★ □*Evita, Goodreads*

"An incredibly beautiful love story that I will never forget." ★★★★★ *Phuong, Goodreads*

"Not all love stories are perfect but they are **real** and everyone wants them." ★★★★★ *Chris, Goodreads*

"This book **touched my heart and soul**." ★★★★★ *Daniela, Goodreads*

"Not many authors would write this kind of romance, but that's why it's **so powerful and so memorable**." ★★★★★ □*Jody, Goodreads*

ABOUT THE AUTHOR

Writing a book was number one on Mari Carr's bucket list. Now her computer is jammed full of stories — novels, novellas, short stories and dead-ends. A *New York Times* and *USA TODAY* bestseller, Mari finds time for writing by squeezing it into the hours between 3 a.m. and daybreak when her family is asleep.

You can visit Mari's website at www.maricarr.com. She is also on Facebook and Twitter.

Look for these titles by Mari Carr

Big Easy:
Blank Canvas
Crash Point
Full Position
Rough Draft
Triple Beat
Winner Takes All
Going Too Fast

Boys of Fall:
Free Agent
Red Zone
Wild Card

Compass:
Northern Exposure
Southern Comfort
Eastern Ambitions
Western Ties
Winter's Thaw
Hope Springs
Summer Fling
Falling Softly
Heaven on Earth
Into the Fire
Still Waters
Light as Air

June Girls:
No Recourse
No Regrets

Just Because:
Because of You
Because You Love Me
Because It's True

Lowell High:
Bound by the Past
Covert Affairs
Mad about Meg

Second Chances:
Fix You
Dare You
Just You
Near You
Reach You
Always You

Sparks in Texas:
Sparks Fly
Waiting for You
Something Sparked
Off Limits
No Other Way
Whiskey Eyes

What Women Want:
Sugar and Spice
Everything Nice

Trinity Masters:
Elemental Pleasure
Primal Passion
Scorching Desire
Forbidden Legacy
Hidden Devotion
Elegant Seduction
Secret Scandal
Delicate Ties
Beloved Sacrifice
Masterful Truth

Masters' Admiralty:
Treachery's Devotion
Loyalty's Betrayal
Pleasure's Fury
Honor's Revenge
Bravery's Sin

Cocktales:
Party Naked
Screwdriver
Bachelor's Bait
Screaming O

Wild Irish:
Come Monday
Ruby Tuesday
Waiting for Wednesday
Sweet Thursday
Friday I'm in Love
Saturday Night Special
Any Given Sunday
Wild Irish Christmas

Wilder Irish:
Wild Passion
Wild Desire
Wild Devotion
Wild at Heart
Wild Temptation
Wild Kisses
Wild Fire
Wild Spirit

Individual Titles:
Seducing the Boss
Tequila Truth
Erotic Research
Rough Cut
Happy Hour

Wild Devotion